The Colours of Sound

Anupam Sen Gupta

PARTRIDGE
A Penguin Random House Company

ISBN:	Hardcover	978-1-4828-4100-8
	Softcover	978-1-4828-4101-5
	eBook	978-1-4828-4099-5

To order additional copies of this book, contact
Partridge India
000 800 10062 62
orders.india@partridgepublishing.com

www.partridgepublishing.com/india

To my family

PREFACE

I grew up in the city of Calcutta, now called Kolkata. My father was a captain in the merchant navy, and I travelled the high seas with him on a cargo ship called the *ISS Indian Resource* in the early 1970s. Those days, ships ran on steam and had a huge number of crew members on board.

Some would play cards while some played the guitar. One young officer very often sang *'Have you ever seen the rain'* by Credence Clearwater Revival in the salon till the butler played the xylophone, indicating that dinner was served.

Officers or their families were *not* allowed to enter the dinning hall in casuals or with wet hair. So I would mostly eat in my father's cabin, as I hated to go down in formals when all I wanted was to sleep.

Life was not much of a problem till 1980 when I forced my mother to buy me a guitar on my twelfth birthday. By then, my father had decided to stop sailing and had set up his own enterprise in Kolkata.

I always wanted to wear the smart stripes on my cuffs with shinning brass buttons on my double-breasted jacket like my father. In school, I only painted ships and the seas.

But my first guitar changed it all. Through a friend's elder brother, I was exposed to some hippie aesthetic music, and I instantly connected. Years went by, and the prodigal son of a respectable family soon became a bit of a nuisance with all the experiments that I did with my life.

Some of my family members had their dreams concerning me. And these dreams were to match the status of the family more than handing over a legacy.

So when I played the blues, formed bands, spent time in *adda* with friends, travelled from village to village with a member of Azad Hind Volunteers, or worked in a couple of early Bengali television soap operas, I made their jumbo jet crash in the family backyard and the skeletons ran inside to hide in the cupboards.

I travelled in and out of relationships, and with each, I matured. My compulsive need to be a rebel led to alcoholism and substance abuse, and my lifestyle was good enough for my family to publicly disown me. By this time, I had lost my father.

As my music didn't give me enough money to survive, I worked in shipping for over a decade with the last being the Head-Freight Marketing and Operations for a maritime agency till one day I decided to *live* for myself. I gave up home, all my money, and all relationships and walked out empty-handed. Actually, it was a *little* more than that!

After a series of events, life brought me to the mountains in North India, where I travelled penniless.

I met some monks and soon accepted monkhood, as I had no choice. This way, I could travel with them to remote places. And also I could find shelter and food.

Spirituality was surely not the reason. Not at least when the stomach rumbled, and in search of nirvana, all I would see were grumpy faces eclipsed by smoke from chillums.

But not all. There were a few. A few who were lost in happiness. Happiness in search of themselves.

Some of them gave me shelter, food, clothing and took care of me when in heavy snow, I almost collapsed, suffering from early stages of frostbite and hypothermia.

I was baptised as a *Naga* by the banks of a turbulent river where I stood stark naked and performed my last rites. My new name was Anu Giri. It was during this time that I met my *guru*. And interestingly, he was not a *Naga*, and I have never met him again after that.

He decoded and deconstructed the magic called 'life' for me. He taught me to love self and love life. I paid my humble tribute to him through a song, which I made with my band members that hit top of the charts in 2002 in India called, *'Funk Monk'* at the *Rock Street Journal Great Indian Rock.*

My mother, after a year and half of search with the help of my aunt and uncle, who was a parliamentarian, found me in the mountains. It was winter, and I had travelled a good 9,000 feet down and was living at that time in a village temple that was a little climb from Vikasnagar.

She asked me if I knew of a monk who played the guitar and was a Bengali called *Anupam* from Kolkata. Needless to say, she didn't recognise me.

I came back with her. It was a weird transitory phase in life. I had shaved my beard off and my head bald. I refused to go back to Kolkata and started living in a *jhuggi jhopdi* in Khanpur in New Delhi. I survived by teaching small kids, who would give me more love than money.

I found a job as an ad hoc junior music teacher in a well-known school, and the only document I had was my passport that had lapsed. And this was around the winters.

I bought myself a pair of faded denims, a couple of shirts, and a pair of shoes from a market opposite the Red Fort that sold used stuff – all for some Rs. 275.

Some senior teachers took serious offence as I walked with my hands in my pockets. Also, I would not wear much warm clothing in the killing winter of Delhi. This too was perceived as a new ad hoc junior teacher trying to make a style statement.

But the fact of the matter was that I didn't have spare money to buy warm clothing, as I had to save to buy a blanket to sleep. The only way to keep myself warm was to keep my hands in the pockets and practise some breathing exercises that I had learnt in the mountains.

Now I live a *'sociably acceptable life'*, drive a fancy car, and have made some investments to secure my family's future. But I find genuine love and compassion only within the warmth of my home unlike a couple of decades ago, when a stranger would share his food and give me shelter in the wilderness of rugged high-altitude mountains never to meet again.

One such person is Chandra Bahadur, who runs a tea stall made of four bamboo poles with a plastic sheet on top, high up in the mountains. He and his wife always shared their food and ensured that I ate at least one meal a day.

Another person is a Frenchman called Pascal, who travelled all the way to the city for days to come back with a guitar for me. The locals after this started calling me the *'Sitarawala Baba'*.

Puran Singh helped me walk from Neelkanth to Badrinath and finally Yamunotri till we trekked up to Saptarishi Kund, which is actually the source of the river Yamuna. We lived in caves, in village temples, in abandoned rooms till one day he disappeared, and I have never met him again till date.

A young man called Bharat was my best friend when I lived around Yamunotri. He would spend all his time with me and travelled with me through heavy snow to far-flung places till I was baptised as a *Naga*. He never spoke to me after that as he felt that I had disowned him. Interestingly, I still haven't figured out the actual meaning of *'Naga'*!

The journey has been tough yet exciting. Tiring yet powerful. Painful yet motivating. Detached yet happy. And I would like to believe that it's just the tip of the iceberg, or else life will become boring.

This collection of short stories is based on my real-life experiences around which I have painted colours of fiction. I have changed names, locations, and timeline and have retained the essence of the actual incidents only, with stories crafted around them.

The idea is simply to share some happenings that influenced my life, and I sum them up as powerful experiences that happen with everybody; some identify them on their own, and some are made to identify them through a series of happenings. That's the fun of nature, I guess!

This book is the first in the series and covers a few such happenings, and I leave you to isolate the truth from fiction.

Any unsolicited resemblance with any living or dead being or place or belief is purely coincidental and is not meant to hurt anybody's sentiments. All characters are fictional.

I hope you enjoy reading the book and request you to leave your thoughts and feedback on the *'The Colours of Sound'* social media pages or you could write to me at *'thecoloursofsound@anupamsengupta.com'* so that I can thank you for your time and effort to read it.

Ferry to Gosaba

Amit and Som were sitting on the top deck of a wooden boat powered by a light engine that navigated her way through the waters of Matla River.

It was a bright sunny winter, and the boat had all sorts of people carrying goats, cycles and baskets full of fish. A fair amount of stink of human sweat was nullified by the fresh air that blew across the river.

On one side, in the distance, there was a thin line of trees and a ferry ghat, and on the other side, there was a thick jungle. The boat travelled below 15 km per hour and blew her horn right into the ears of Amit and Som.

Smaller boats powered by the strength of human arms and oars kept distance from the larger one, chugging her way through the waters.

Unlike many black-and-white movies, no boatman was singing any song. There was no *'Oh Maji'* by S. D. Burman. Instead, the wheelhouse, in which the supervisor incessantly smoked *biris*, had a tape deck with a single speaker that blew the eardrums with songs from latest Hindi blockbusters.

The boat had started her journey from Basanti. Basanti is about 100 km from the City of Joy and takes nearly two and a half hours by state transport buses from Babu Ghat.

Amit and Som were close friends, who had embarked on a journey from Kolkata to Gosaba. Amit wanted to visit the island as he had heard about an organisation called Azad Volunteers who were working 'mysteriously' towards the development of the otherwise backward island.

Som had a job to do. He had the contract of installing a dish antenna in the only local police station in the remote island in the Sundarbans.

Gosaba was a strategic British army base during the Second World War against the Japanese. But it is of no surprise that after so many years of independence, this area remains to be one of the most remote places in Gangetic Bengal.

The year 1991 – it was 6 December.

By 5 p.m., both friends had landed on the banks of Gosaba. The boat almost ran aground on the muddy bank of the island. A wooden plank was thrown across from the starboard side of the boat to the flight of stairs that was the gateway to the island.

Amit and Som balanced their way on the plank and climbed the stairs into a makeshift yet busy market. The sun was tired and was preparing to go down.

The friends found a tea stall by a large playground and asked for *chai* and some *nimkis*. Som knew where to go, but Amit was a bit clueless. He had only heard stories about Azad Volunteers. So before it was too late, he donned the hat of Holmes and started his investigation.

Amit asked the tea stall vendor if he knew anything about such an organisation that was working towards the upliftment of the area. The vendor preferred to be busy rather answer Amit's question. Before Amit could shoot the next question, Som paid and asked for the direction to the police station. Such contradiction in the questions asked by the friends didn't seem to surprise the tea vendor a bit.

The sun was lazily going down the horizon, and on the other side the moon was visible in the sky. They walked along the banks through a narrow path that flirted its way through the beautiful view of the wide river without any sign of land as far as the eye could see and some 'view-obstructing shacks', which had huge weighing scales. It seemed that they were used for bulk trading of fish caught by the fisherman of the island.

Suddenly out of the darkness, there appeared a young man who had a huge torch in his hand. He was going the same way and was willing to show Som the direction to the police station.

Amit didn't waste time to get into a conversation with the stranger. With the moonlight falling on the face of the stranger, Amit realised that this young man was also having tea a while back in the same stall and had overheard the entire conversation between them and the tea vendor.

'What brings you here?' the stranger asked.

Som quickly took control and said that he had to install a dish antenna at the police station.

'When do you plan to go back?' asked the stranger.

'Tomorrow morning,' replied Som.

'You cant,' said the stranger much to the discomfort of both the friends. They thought they were about to be mugged.

'There is a communal tension all over the country,' said the stranger, looking at Amit.

'Communal tension . . . what nonsense!' Amit opposed him firmly.

'That's the police station on your right. See you.' The stranger disappeared in the darkness with only the spotlight of his torch visible.

The journey had made both Amit and Som tired, and the hint of salt in the air told them that the ocean was not far.

Both entered the police station, which had just two rooms with a couple of tables and a wooden cupboard. The lights were depressingly dim, and there was a long bench outside the rooms under a shade made of asbestos that could fall any time.

There were five people, most in the khaki trousers of their uniform and a *shawl* wrapped around while one of them was in a lungi and a heavy pullover.

They were intensely watching television and were having a real rough time with the transmission going off a few times. The man in the lungi noticed the strangers and asked if they were there for the installation of the dish antenna.

'Can you install it right now?' asked the man. 'Humanity is up in flames . . .'

'Up in flames?' Amit asked.

'When did you arrive? Don't you know some mosque has been demolished in Ayodhya, and there is a great amount of plundering and rioting that is happening all over?' informed the man who was the head of the police station.

'What . . . when did all this happen?' Som looked extremely hassled.

'A few hours back. Even Basanti has not been spared. We believe there has been some serious communal tension in the ferry town as well.' The man now almost scared the daylights out of Som.

Basanti was from where Amit and Som had taken a ferry to the island of Gosaba a few hours back after a long bus journey from Babu Ghat in Kolkata.

Now this was getting serious, and the stranger was not wrong! And nor was he trying to mug them!

Som quickly assembled the dish antenna, and with the help of a couple of policemen and Amit, he went up on the asbestos roof!

Amit being the heavier guy, he stayed down and helped Som with the cables. In about half an hour, in the darkness of the night that was filled with apprehensions, Som tuned the receiver and the television, and after a couple of attempts, it started working fine. It was a small-screen black-and-white television but good enough at that point to tune in for the latest news.

The historical Babri Mosque in Ayodhya was demolished by thousands of *kar sevaks*. The situation was grim.

Amidst all this, Amit hesitantly asked, 'Is there some activity by Azad Volunteers on this island?'

'Yeah, I know you were inquiring about them at the tea stall . . . (pause) . . . wait.' And the policeman called out for some Munna.

In walked in the stranger who had first broken the news of communal tension in the country to them. The policeman introduced the stranger as Munna, who was an active volunteer of the 'mysterious' organisation Amit was looking for.

The country was hit by communal disharmony. The cops knew about his intention, and he was accompanied by a stranger who was a member of the organisation. What was all this about?

Amit had heard about the organisation from a social activist from Kanthi in West Bengal. He had heard of a mysterious man called Azad, who led the organisation and would travel from village to village in remote parts of India and empower people to take up self-development. The organisation was peaceful yet had hues of anti-establishment.

Amit was intrigued about the man and wanted to meet him. It was this strong desire that got him to the remote island of Gosaba.

Som stayed back in the police station while Amit and Munna walked out to navigate through the darkness that had fallen on the region. In a few minutes, they were back at the tea stall. The tea vendor almost seemed to be waiting for them. He looked like a silhouette painting against the moonlight.

It didn't take Amit too much of time to figure out that his interests and movements were being monitored. And not from the time he reached the island but from the time he had decided to come. The social activist from Kanthi was a member of the organisation and knew when Amit was travelling to Gosaba, and he had informed who needed to be informed.

The tea vendor, Munna, and Amit went across the large playground to a shack. The light was dim in the shack and had some fifty-odd people who had flocked outside it. There was an elderly frail man sitting next to a small radio and giving updates to the people who had flocked.

Munna took Amit inside the shack. The old man asked him to sit next to him. The news on air was spine-chilling. Mankind was being torn apart by strong communal violence.

The elderly man put the radio off and walked out of the shack. He rolled a newspaper like a microphone and updated the people who had flocked outside.

By this time, Som and the head policeman came in and joined the crowd. The policeman whispered something into the ears of the elderly man.

The elderly man asked for a stool. Munna was quick to get one from inside. He stood on it with the help of Munna and the tea vendor.

Amit and Som looked at each other and had no other option.

The elderly man asked the crowd to get back to their homes and quickly come back with iron rods, sticks, and whatever they could get their hands on which could work as weapon of self-defence.

Som was trembling and so was Amit. Was the elderly man preparing for some kind of violence on the island?

On the stool stood this frail man with the makeshift microphone in hand.

'In the name of Azad, let us all pledge safety for all beings on this island.' With that, the crowd reciprocated the old man with a large cry.

Amit was scared but also thrilled. It was an experience that he was not expecting.

'Make groups of five. Pick up all that you can. Be responsible. Block all in roads to the island. Block all exit routes. Block all ferry ghats. We must not have any untoward incident on the island of Gosaba . . . some groups take the responsibility of patrolling around the residential areas . . . Some of you, please take your cycles and rush to Rangabelia. Get people together there and block all in roads to the island . . .' The elderly frail man stepped down from the stool and went back inside the dimly lit shack.

While the crowd hurried out to take care of their respective responsibilities given out, the elderly man, turned the radio on for more news. He looked grim. Worried. Concerned.

Som, Amit, and the policeman were asked to join him. The tea vendor stood outside the shack with Munna, armed with iron rods.

The conversation that followed between the elderly man and the policeman clearly gave a sense that the people of the island were closely connected with each other and would not let any bit of the communal violence reach them. News started coming in that people of close-by islands were traumatised by the fear of unpleasant happenings.

The elderly man had tears rolling down his checks yet was burning with anger.

'How can anybody destroy a piece of history in the name of religion? How can anybody be so insensitive to the sentiments of either communities . . . goons . . . bloody goons are on the streets of the country killing innocent people in the name of religion.' The old man trembled, clenching his fists.

It was already 11 p.m. Some policemen who were watching news joined in with their rifles. They met the senior policeman and were instructed to guard the main ferry ghat. The boat in which Som and Amit came was still there but now the mudbank was filled with the rising water of the tide. There was no change in how the moon looked, and with night getter deeper, it was getting really cold.

The elderly man asked Som where he was putting up for the night. The head policeman intervened and said that Amit and Som could sleep in the police station, and both could have their meals there with the men on duty.

Amit was in no mood to sleep – and that too when people of the island were patrolling and guarding roads to protect her from any communal violence. He insisted that he join the men to protect the island.

The elderly man didn't oppose him but told Amit in a very *Kabiresque* way that no war can be fought or religion be practised with an empty stomach. He instructed Munna to take him home, and after a quick dinner, both could go and guard the entry to the village.

So both friends went different ways in the middle of the night with news pouring in from all parts of the land of terrible violence.

While walking towards Munna's home in the cold night, Amit had to quench his thirst about the 'mysterious' man who headed the Azad Volunteers. Amit had no questions about the activities and the integrity of the organisation. He had just witnessed what the organisation stood for.

'Swamiji suddenly appeared on the island one day. The area was hit by a huge cyclone that destroyed homes and killed a few boatmen in sea who couldn't return in time . . . Since that day, he has got people of the island together and has also involved all agencies like the police and even local politicians to get on one platform towards the betterment of all of us who have been struggling against nature and life to survive,' said Munna.

There was immense amount of belief and emotion that backed every little word Munna said.

Munna opened a gate made of bamboo. A lady walked up with her head covered with her sari. They both welcomed Amit and offered him water to drink and wash his hands.

In all the chaos, Amit hadn't had water for hours now and drank as much as he could. The lady, Munna's wife, led them into the mud hut that had a thatched roof. It had a door, which even a strong wind could break open. Inside there were two rooms.

She laid out two banana leaves on the floor. Amit and Munna had dinner together. The meal was simple, and it seemed that the lady had just cooked the rice and the daal a moment back.

It was 1 a.m. The sky was clear, and the winds made it even colder.

Munna took two blankets. He gave one to Amit and with the other, he wrapped himself. While the lady locked the door, both men walked out with iron rods in their hands.

The night passed without a single incidence of violence on the island. The morning was cold, and the wide river on her way to the ocean was engulfed with fog.

Birds took time to chirp, and the sun took his time to come out. It was what winter is expected to be like in the Sunderbans. Around 8 a.m., the shack that housed the office of Azad Volunteers had a crowd, a crowd of people who protected the island from any mishap through the cold winter night.

By 10 a.m., the group that had gone to Rangabelia came back. By this time women too had gathered, the crowd swelling to a good hundred-odd people.

The elderly man came out of the shack and went around hugging people. He asked Munna to tell everybody to go home and rest while the women could take positions. He also instructed that since people in Rangabelia had taken control, there was not much to worry. Also, beyond the river after Rangabelia was Sojnekhali Tiger Reserve. So the fear was that of tigers more than men.

The sun by this time was bright. The sky was clear. The radio was on in the shack while the television was on in the police station.

Women took positions to protect the island while the men went home to rest.

The head policeman and Som came hurriedly to the shack and looked for Amit. Amit had gone to Munna's home to catch some sleep. Munna's wife had left some food for the men and was out with an iron rod in her hand with other women to protect the island from any communal violence.

Som tried contacting his home in Kolkata to inform that both the friends were safe and would return after the violence calmed down a bit. But the communication system in the police station had failed, and Som was worried about people at home.

The tidal waters had receded by then. The boats sat on the mudbank with the waters coming and touching the keels only to go back again.

The fog had cleared. In the distance, a few container feeder vessels could be seen. They were anchored mid-river, probably on the advice of their agents to avoid entering the ports of Haldia and Kolkata till the tension was in control.

The newscasters, both on radio and television, were getting choked reading out breaking news. It was a terrible moment for the people of land.

Ayodhya was completely taken over by the *kar sevaks*. They tied bandanas on their heads, and some now say, they even had gunpowder to blow up serious concrete structures.

The historical monument of *Babri Mosque* was destroyed to dust. History was being written with the tears of the people, the colour of which was red. The stench of pain engulfed the subcontinent.

On the other hand, five days had passed with not a single bit of violence on the island of Gosaba. Army was out in the rest of the country, and the situation was gradually settling down.

Som and Amit decided to get back home via Canning, which is on the other side of the river and had less reporting of crime and hatred, but due to the extreme nature of the violence around the country, no ferry was plying.

And from Canning, they planned to catch a local train and enter the city of Kolkata, which was still under curfew.

The moment came when Amit and Som were to part from the people of the island. A ferry was going to Canning as some people of Gosaba were stuck there and had to be brought back. Some twenty people had come to see them off at the ferry ghat. It was an emotional moment for all. They all had collectively survived the disastrous massacre without one single scar on the island.

Amit was going back as the ambassador of the Azad Volunteers that his urban South Kolkata friends had no clue about. Nor did the media. Som set up the first dish antenna on the island.

Just before the launch was about to sail, Amit ran to Munna and gave him a hug. Both were emotionally charged.

Amit wanted to keep in touch and wanted Munna's details. Munna got a piece of paper and a pen from the ferry supervisor and requested Amit to write as he couldn't read or write.

'Name: Munnaf........ Village: Gosaba . . .' Before he could complete, Amit stopped writing and looked at Munna in utter disbelief. Munna and his wife never let Amit feel even once that they were of a different religion in case he would feel insecure.

Amit and Som boarded the launch. It sailed, navigating through the numerous water bodies on her way to Canning. Amit stood on the deck looking at Gosaba in disbelief. Munna stood still on the banks till the launch went out of sight.

Amit had no clue about the 'mysterious' man who could create such sense of cohesiveness in a backward remote island in the deltaic region, though the footprints of great leadership of Azad were visible in the people of the island of Gosaba.

While people of the land hung their heads in shame on 6 December 1991, Gosaba created history that will probably never be written, and nobody will ever know anything about Azad!

GHOOMAR

The wide road between the entrance to Meena Bazar at the foot of Jama Masjid and Red Fort has a divider. The divider works as home to many. Mostly drug addicts and petty thieves.

Amongst them lived Nand Lal and Pagla Sai.

Nand Lal was born blind in Mathura to a local fabric merchant. His father had come to Chadni Chowk, Delhi, when Nand Lal was six years old to buy fabric in bulk and left him to his fate as a blind son was no more than a liability.

He was seen crying by a police constable and was finally sent to a juvenile reformatory home. Nand Lal grew up there but ran away at the age of fifteen. Since then, he has lived on the streets around Meena Bazar and Red Fort area in Delhi.

Pagla Sai was extremely temperamental, had traits of eccentricity, and spoke Urdu fluently. His actual name was Maqsood Khan and was originally a resident of Kashmere Gate in Delhi.

Maqsood walked out of his home after he handed over his three-storeyed house and a prosperous business of automobile spare parts to his two sons. He was tired of regular unpleasant scenes at home between the brothers and their wives.

Both met when they had queued up for food that was being distributed by a charity in Chadni Chowk on a cold winter day. Nand Lal was pushed out of the queue by some young drug addicts. Pagla Sai chased the boys away and helped Nand Lal back to the queue. Since then, both had been friends.

Even though they lived on the streets braving the scorching summers and extreme cold winters, they never begged. They lived off food that was either distributed by charity or ate at the *langar* in a nearby gurdwara.

Nand Lal was a great singer and an extremely soft person by nature, while Maqsood was aggressive. He would chase young boys and girls who would come to buy heroin from the drug peddlers in the middle of the night.

One Diwali night, when the Delhi sky was lit with random bursts of crackers, a dark man in his mid-forties came in a *pagdi* wearing *juttis,* thick silver anklets, and dhoti till his knees and sat next to them.

The man asked Pagla Sai if he could give him some food to eat and mentioned that he had not eaten in the last forty-eight hours. Nand Lal had a couple of puris that he had saved. So he handed them over.

'You don't seem to be from Delhi,' asked Pagla Sai.

'No . . . I am not. I come from the foothills of the Aravalis, from a remote village called Dhumra. I am a Bhil,' answered the man.

'You have come looking for a job?' asked Nand Lal.

'Who will give me a job?' asked the man.

'What's your name?' probed Pagla Sai.

With the night getting deeper and deeper, the sky was getting more and more lit with colourful firecrackers.

'My name is Bhimisi, and I am a *mandno* artist with no work and a large family to feed back home,' the man shared his ordeal.

'Our area is dry and barren. The panchayat had received money twice to dig a canal so that we could get water and till our land to survive, but all the money disappeared . . . Some people became very rich and migrated out of the area, while we are dying with no job, no food, no land to till . . . Last year, before elections, politicians came to our village and promised electricity. What do we do with electricity when we have no food to eat . . .,' continued the stranger.

Pagla Sai lit three *biris* and gave one to Nand Lal and one to the stranger. The night was getting chilly and Pagla Sai lit some cardboard boxes that he had gathered.

With the night sky filled with smog and lit with firecrackers, the three slept off next to the remains of the fire Pagla Sai had lit.

The next morning, the sun couldn't smile on the people who needed him the most as the city was engulfed in a thick layer of smog. The roads were littered with leftover of firecrackers. Diwali was over.

Pagla Sai woke up first. He looked extremely thoughtful. He woke up Nand Lal and took him about twenty feet away.

'Nandu . . . I have been thinking about this for a while now . . . Our lives can't go waste. We need to do something meaningful that makes our lives worthwhile. Let's go to Bhimisi's village and see how we can help them,' asserted Pagla Sai.

'What? . . . How? . . . What can we do?' asked a shocked Nand Lal.

'Nandu, I have saved my last reserve for the past two decades. When I left home, I kept my marriage ring with me and decided that I would use it at the most critical juncture in my life . . . I think the time has come, and the call from within is to do something worthwhile with our otherwise useless lives,' replied Pagla Sai.

The plan that followed was to sell the solitaire-studded gold ring and with the money go to Bhimisi's village. Pagla Sai knew what to do till here but had no clue about what to do at the village. But he was determined to make their own lives meaningful.

They shared the plan with Bhimisi, whose first reaction was shock. What could homeless people do for people who were struggling to survive in a tough and barren region with no money, no job, and no food?

But Bhimisi didn't have much of a choice, and the three embarked on a journey to uncertainty. It was after an overnight train journey followed by a long bus travel and then walk for hours that the three reached the village.

The land was parched, and the entire area was so dusty that they had to keep their faces covered. Bhimisi's house had six members and was a mud hut with a thatched roof with one room that had cracked badly. Male members slept outside on *charpai* while the women and children struggled to fit themselves in the small hut.

Pagla Sai and Nand Lal found shelter in a nearby Shitala Devi temple, which had a tube well and was the only source of fresh water in the village.

'How far is the river?' asked Pagla Sai.

'It should be about ten to twelve miles away,' said Bhimisi.

'And who owns the land in between the river and your village?' inquired Pagla Sai.

'Nobody . . . it's completely barren. Even grass doesn't grow in the soil,' informed Bhimisi.

The plan for the next day was to walk to the river. At the crack of dawn, they set out through the dry and barren land in the direction of the river.

By midday, they were by the banks after having crossed ten villages.

Pagla Sai, hungry and tired, sat next to the banks and contemplated. After an hour, he suggested that the people of all the villages should get together and dig a canal that could carry water from the river to Dhumra. While doing this, all the villages en route would get water and would be able to till some portions of the otherwise useless land for survival.

Bhimisi thought this was a non-starter and took out six bajra rotis that his wife had packed for their journey to the river. While Nand Lal and Bhimisi ate, Pagla Sai kept looking at the waters.

The sun was going down. It was really cold. Bhimisi suggested that they walk back to Dhumra and discuss Pagla Sai's idea with the rest of the villagers and come back to the river another day. Bhimisi realised that coming back from Delhi with these men was a mistake.

Pagla Sai suddenly noticed a small concrete structure by the river. He walked towards it and opened the rickety tin door. There were construction tools inside that had gathered dust and rust.

'That's the only thing that happened in the name of the canal,' informed Bhimisi.

'*Bhai,* you carry on . . . We shall stay back.' Pagla Sai asked Bhimisi to go back.

After a bit of an agreement and disagreement, Bhimisi went ahead and Nand Lal and Pagla Sai stayed back by the river.

The sun was gradually going down. The friends went inside the storeroom and cleaned a bit of space for both to spend the night.

The night passed. Both men shivered in the cold. At the crack of dawn, Pagla Sai woke Nand Lal and told him that he needn't worry too much as he was still left with more than Rs. 35,000 with him from the sale of his wedding ring.

Days passed. Bhimisi had not heard from the men from Delhi and wanted to check if they were still there. So he walked for hours crossing village after village and reached the river.

To his surprise there was a temple with triangular red and orange flags at the place of the construction store site. People flocked to the temple; there were a few tea vendors and one stall that sold sweets and flowers for puja.

'What is this? When did this happen?' he asked himself as he went closer.

When he arrived at the door of the new temple, he was completely taken aback seeing Nand Lal and Pagla Sai dressed as sanyasis. Nand Lal was singing bhajans while Pagla Sai sat in deep meditation.

'Baba says that this entire land is full of treasures. There is money buried in the land from here to Dhumra. The footprints of a great saint who walked on this land about a century ago have turned into coins. Since the people have turned this stretch of land into shitting fields, Gods have become angry,' updated another villager.

'What?' asked a shocked Bhimisi.

'Baba says that if we don't clean the land and stop using it for shitting all over, we shall all die . . . And the digging for treasure will begin from Makar Sankranti . . . about two months away. Any digging before that will bring curse on us . . . till then Baba will not talk,' added the villager.

Chants of '*Jai Baba Pagla Sai*' filled the air.

Poor Bhimisi walked back to his village and shared the story with a couple of villagers, who decided to go back to the temple the next morning and confront Pagla Sai in public.

The next afternoon, when they arrived, some locals were sitting by the bank of the river. Bhimisi and his people called them and told them about his encounter with these men in Delhi and how they got here. In all the chaos and shouting, a few more people got together from the nearby village.

Pagla Sai sat in meditation while Nand Lal sang bhajans.

Bhimisi came forward and called both a fraud.

Suddenly Pagla Sai jumped out of the temple and started cursing the people.

'You have disturbed my mediation . . . You will all suffer . . . You are such morons that you don't even know that you are standing on a pot of treasure . . . Dig the place right now,' shouted Pagla Sai.

By this time more and more people had gathered.

Bhimisi and a couple of people started digging, and in about ten minutes, they found a copper vessel with 200 one-rupee coins.

Suddenly the air was filled with euphoric chants of *'Jai Baba Pagla Sai'*.

The locals chased Bhimisi and his village men away and fell at Pagla Sai's feet and begged for forgiveness.

He quietly went back and sat in meditation, but before that he asked that the copper pot with the coins be given to Bhimisi.

Word spread like wildfire, and from then on people from far and near started coming to see Pagla Sai, and with that came offerings and money.

Weeks passed. Months passed and then came the pious day of Makar Sankranti. Hundreds of people gathered to witness the miracle.

Pagla Sai quietly came out of the temple. Looked around. Bhimisi was standing right in front with folded hands.

'I have marked the land with *sindoor* that you should dig for treasure. It's marked from here to Dhumra. All the money collected must be distributed between villages that fall in this path from Bhimisi's village to the river . . .' And Pagla Sai walked back inside the temple. Nand Lal started singing bhajans.

Amidst chants of *'Jai Baba Pagla Sai'*, the villagers stated digging. And to everybody's surprise, at every thirty to fifty feet they found copper pots with a few one-rupee coins. The more they found, the heavier the chants grew.

This carried on for two days; while Pagla Sai patiently sat in meditation, Nand Lal sang bhajans.

After two days, the villagers had dug almost a canal from the banks of the river to Bhimisi's village. The village heads came in the evening with folded hands and all the money collected.

Pagla Sai emerged from the temple and said that it was time for him to leave. He instructed that the money be divided among all the villages that fell in the path of the treasure hunt and be used to dig the canal a little more and create a concrete dam at the point where it met the river.

'God is pleased, and so am I. From this monsoon, your lives will change. You will grow crops. You will have money, and you will be happy,' blessed Pagla Sai.

He told the villagers that he would leave the next morning.

Amidst heavy winter fog, at the crack of dawn, Pagla Sai and Nand Lal stepped out of the temple. They handed the temple over to Bhimisi and asked him to keep the devi pleased by starting a small school for children.

The air was filled with chants of '*Jai Baba Pagla Sai*'. In celebration, women started dancing *ghoomar* – an original Bhil dance form that is performed during the month of *Shravan* and has now been adapted by others across states and communities.

Both men walked up to Bhimisi and hugged him.

'Jai Baba Pagla Sai,' shouted the villager.

'Bhimisi, in the eyes of the world, I am mad . . . but in my eyes, the entire world is mad,' laughed Pagla Sai as they walked away from the celebrations into the thick fog of high winters.

TAWAIF

Vasiq's family had migrated to London when he was two. The rest of his extended family lived in Aminabad in the heritage city of Lucknow.

Vasiq would visit India once in five years for a week with his family. As a child he hardly had any connect with the city where he was born. He had grown up as a fine young Englishman and was completing his research in prenatal genetics.

They lived on Elmstead Close in Totteridge in North London. His father, Dr Parvez Naqvi, was an orthodontist, who preferred to be called Vezvi.

Well, Dr Vezvi had never administered one single injection in India and believed that with independence, the country had lost her opportunity to be civilised. On the contrary, he did a lot of charity work in East End and around Tilbury. He would volunteer as a doctor for the immigrant port workers, which earned him a lot of reputation in the stiff upper-lip communities whom he idolised.

Vasiq had a creative bent of mind and was keen to explore Awadhi culture and his roots, much to the annoyance of his father.

He would often visit Hyde Park's Speakers' Corner. One bright summer Sunday, he saw an elderly gentleman who was reading out poetry from his collections with almost no audience. What attracted him was that this gentleman was wearing a well-ironed white kurta with *chikankari* on it and a *kashti numa topi*.

The gentleman's attire looked like what Vasiq's grandfather wore during Eid when he was on a trip to England over a decade back.

Though Vasiq couldn't understand one single bit of the poems, it seemed so close to what his grandfather would speak like in Urdu.

So Vasiq waited for the gentleman to be free. It was late afternoon. Vasiq went and introduced himself and shared his interest to understand what the gentleman had to say.

The conversation led to the city of Lucknow, and Vaisq realised that the gentleman, Dildaar Lakhnawi, was trying to promote Urdu poetry while he was on a trip to meet his daughter, who lived in Willow End, which was at a right angle to Elmstead Close where Vasiq lived.

Both met again over tea at Willow End. Vasiq wanted to know more about Lucknow and expressed his desire to explore the culture and his roots. The gentleman shared Udru couplets and translated in immaculate English for Vasiq to comprehend.

That evening was a turning point in Vasiq's life; it ended with the gentleman reciting works by Anees, Dabeer, Shauq, and Josh.

The young research scholar walked back home with the works of the seventeenth-century poet Sheikh Imam Baksh Nasikh Lakhnawi resonating in his mind.

Aasmaan ki kya hai taaqat, jo churrae Lakhnau,

Lakhnau mujh per fida hai, Main fida-e-Lakhnau!

(*What strength does heaven have that it can steal Lakhnau from me; I am in love with her, and she is with me.*)

Next morning, Vasiq went to Totteridge Green and sat for hours at the Totteridge Cricket Club Ground under an oak tree while young boys practised in the distance.

He was convinced that he had to visit Lucknow and spend time in his hometown. Vasiq had to get back to his roots.

Months passed. He spent most of his time studying about Lucknow and her culture. Just before winter was about to set in in London, Vasiq bought a ticket to India from his stipend.

Dr Vezvi was terribly annoyed, but that couldn't stop the pull of the umbilical cord in Vasiq.

His grandfather was very old and hardly could see but was very happy to welcome his grandson and so was the extended family. For the first few days, it was spending evenings at Hazratgunj with his cousins and lavish dinners in traditional style on *takaht* at home.

Vasiq loved the way *khasa dastarkhwan* that the *khansamas* laid out every night before he got tired of the *mehman nawazi* and wanted to live like anybody else in the family.

Vasiq got friendly with Talea Azma Naqvi, his first cousin who ran a photo-framing shop in Picture Lane in Aminabad. Vasiq preferred to call him Jaanbaaz.

Jaanbaaz and Vasiq visited the older parts of the city and met people who were still holding on to their culture and lineage. They walked through the lanes of Chowk with the growing rhythmic sounds of wooden hammers of the artisans making *vark* with the essence of musk in the air coming from *ittar* shops at Akbari Gate.

Vasiq had read about *tawaifs* and could feel the resonance of *ghungroos* and *tumri* between his ears whenever he walked the old alleys of the city of nawabs.

One evening, at Jaanbaaz's shop sipping a hot cup of tea, Vasiq expressed his desire to meet a *tawaif*.

'Brother . . . you are inviting trouble. But if you are interested, I know where to go.' Jaanbaaz winked.

Next evening, both the cousins went to the older part of the city. They walked through a complex network of narrow lanes and then climbed a staircase leading up to a large room with a high ceiling that had skylights and not a single window.

Decadence of erstwhile aristocracy was visible all over. In the corner sat an elderly lady on a chair that seemed to be worthy of a royalty.

Jaanbaaz exchanged pleasantries and asked if Vasiq could meet Ada. He explained that Vasiq had travelled all the way from England to study the history of *tawaifs*.

The lady was initially reluctant but agreed for this young pretty woman to walk out of the *cheekh*.

The young lady came and sat right opposite Jaanbaaz and asked, 'This is not a *kotha* . . . it's our home. What *else* can I do for you, *janab*?'

Jaanbaaz had to reconfirm and reassure her that his cousin wanted to study the heritage of *tawaifs* and that was the sole purpose of his visit.

A long conversation began.

The lady shared that the house that she lived in was given as a gift to her ancestor by Nawab Wajid Ali Shah, who had a keen interest in *kathak, ghazals, thumri,* and other arts.

Ada was the last *tawaif* in their lineage and was hired to do *mujras* at parties hosted by the rich and the influential all over India. With this she was able to earn a decent living, but it was not good enough to maintain a large family of young brothers, an ailing mother, and an ancestral haveli.

She added, '*Tawaifs* were courtesans who particularly catered to the nobility and excelled in various forms of art, including theatre. Interestingly, they were considered authorities in etiquette or *tahzeeb*. Nobilities would send their growing male members of the house to them to learn etiquette.'

Ada looked angry as she continued. The lady on the chair kept a watch on the conversation from a distance.

Ada was not exquisitely dressed and did not have loud make-up. She wore a white well-ironed salwar kameez and had her head covered with a light green *chunni*. The only ornamentation was a nose pin and dark *kajal* that made her large eyes look prominent and beautiful against her fair complexion.

Her hands were elegant with well-manicured nails that were not 'painted', and so was her language.

'We took arts to high standards and popularised various dance and music forms. Growing sons of nobilities would be tutored by us to appreciate art,' explained Ada.

She continued, 'It was a medieval tradition that was "bastardised" to prostitution with the annexation of Awadh by the British in 1856.'

Vasiq was completely taken aback. He didn't have much to say or ask.

'Sadly . . . (pause) in Urdu, the term has undergone semantic pejoration and is now synonymous with a sex worker . . . (pause) . . . and truthfully speaking, we are prostitutes today. After *mujras* at various parties, we have to sleep with the host while their wives keep themselves occupied with various other interests,' sighed Ada with the corners of her eyes getting wet.

Vasiq was getting choked with emotions. Trying to gulp spasms around his throat, he requested Ada for some water.

There was pin drop silence in the room. Ada looked into Vasiq's eyes and turned to Jaanbaaz and the lady on the chair.

'Are you sure?' she asked.

An astonished Vasiq hesitantly replied, 'Yes . . . I mean, I am a bit thirsty'.

An old man with white beard walked out from the room inside. He had *surma* in his eyes and wore a *keffiyeh.*

'*Janab* . . . water.'

He was carrying a large silver tray, and the glasses too were made of silver with very nice carving work on them.

'Will you give only water to the *mehman*? . . . Give them the sweets which Qureshi *Saab* sent over in the morning,' instructed the lady on the chair.

While leaving, the old lady walked to Vasiq. She had tears in her eyes and tried touching his head as a gesture to bless him.

'*Beta,* people today sleep with *tawaifs* but never drink water in their houses, *kotahs* . . . of their hands . . . We are good to sleep with but dirty otherwise.' With this the lady turned back and went inside.

The brothers climbed down the stairs and navigated out of the complex network of alleys to the main road. They stood in front the great *Imambara* which looked like a silhouette painting against the moonlight.

'I hear how *tawaifs* in Hindi movies are usually shown as sex workers who break homes with *kothas* on top of Benarasi paan shops; with the hero drinking and spending nights with her,' commented Vasiq while walking down Laxman Tila in search of a rickshaw.

'They used to, but now the modern-day prostitutes are shown as dusky and voluptuous female executives, models, actors with curly hair with few buttons of their white shirts open...... who are willing to sleep to succeed in life . . . for fame, for money . . . and whatever,' disgustedly added Jaanbaaz.

Both walked quietly for some time.

In the next twenty days, Vasiq explored Lucknow, Faizabad, and a few villages in between the two cities before going back home on Elmstead Close in Totteridge.

He carried on with his research, completed his doctorate, and got a high-paying job as a research scientist in London.

Vasiq spoke to Jaanbaaz once in a while, and that was the time when he felt the pull of the umbilical cord with his roots getting stronger.

Time passed, and it was almost ten months since he had come back from India.

The entire family got extremely busy making arrangements for Vasiq's younger sister's wedding with an English doctor practising in Birmingham. Members of the family were coming in from India, and Dr Vezvi wanted to do whatever he could to make the wedding memorable.

The marriage ceremony happened both in a Protestant Church and at home following Islamic rites, where the groom gave a sedan as gift and ten thousand sterling pounds as *mehr*.

The Naqvi household was jubilant, and Vasiq was very happy to meet Jaanbaaz, who had travelled internationally for the first time.

Dr Vezvi had hired a community hall for a private party for only the members of the bride's and the groom's families.

Just after the newly-wed couple took a break from meeting people, Dr Vezvi took the microphone and announced that he had a surprise entertainment for all.

The lights were dimmed. The floor was cleared. Mattresses were laid out on the sides with white sheets and thick maroon satin pillows with tassels. All the guests were requested to settle on the mattresses while a few musicians in *shervani* and *kashti numa topi* sat on one side with a harmonium, sarangi, tabla and a tanpura.

The huge community hall reverberated with the sounds of *ghungroos*. The central chandelier was lit up. The makeshift display of hundreds of mirrors on the walls lit up the entire room like thousands of diamonds.

At the centre stood a woman – gorgeously dressed; her face was covered with a veil. A beautiful *alaap* filled the air supported by heart-rending sound of the sarangi.

A blue spotlight focused on her as the audience clapped in sheer excitement. The *dadra* on the tabla and the *ghungroo*s synced with the movements of her feet.

She took the veil off, her head still facing down. She moved the hair from her face with another mild spotlight falling on it. A headset microphone coming from behind her head looked almost lost in paradise in front of her lips that she was mockingly biting.

The performance began. It was Ada.

The air was filled with sounds of jubilation. The guests threw money at her in appreciation, much to the annoyance of the English guests. Dr Vezvi had to explain that it was customary and was in appreciation of the art. So, soon they also started throwing money too.

Vasiq stood in one corner. Shocked. Unable to react. Jaanbaaz stood next to him. Ada playfully came to Vasiq and looked into his eyes deeply before pulling him in the performance arena to dance with her.

He shook his hand off and walked out to the smoking zone. Jaanbaaz followed him, but Vasiq looked annoyed and stopped him.

All through the performance, Vasiq stood in the balcony from where he went back home.

Early morning, he was woken up by Jaanbaaz. 'Ada wants to meet you before she takes her flight back to India. She needs a favour from you.'

'So, *Bhai Jaan*, you knew about *Abba's* plan. You knew about Ada coming here to do a *mujra*!' Vasiq fumed.

They both walked down to the guest house adjoining the community hall where Ada and her musicians were put up.

Jaanbaaz knocked the door.

The door opened. Ada stood in a white well-ironed salwar kameez, and her head was covered with a light-green *chunni.* Her eyes looked beautiful with *kajal* defining the depth in them against her fair complexion.

'*Adaab . . . Janab,* please come, if I may,' she invited both to come in.

'So you must be happy having mocked me in public,' asked an angry Vasiq.

Ada smiled and said, 'What to do? It's my job to entertain people.'

'Can you please do me a small favour?' requested the pretty woman.

She walked to the room inside and came back with a small well-packed wooden box. She opened it and took out an idol of Goddess Durga sitting on a lion with her *trishul* well inside the chest of *Mahisasura.*

'I got this on a request for a friend who is a Hindu . . . (looking at the idol) . . . It's devi *puja* for them. I ordered this from Kumortoli in Kolkata. Day after is the beginning of *Navratras.* If you don't have any religious reservations, can I please leave this with you so that she can collect it from your house either today or tomorrow . . . Or else I have to leave it at the reception here,' requested Ada.

Vasiq was a man with liberal thoughts. He agreed immediately.

While she packed the idol back in the wooden box, she looked into Vasiq's eyes and said, 'Idols of Goddess Durga for worship are made of a clay mixture that is incomplete if a portion of the clay doesn't come from a brothel.'

'And come to think of it, people of all religions, castes, and creeds come to brothels. It's probably the only place where there is no communal intolerance. People of all religions sleep with each other. One to satisfy the hunger above the waistline and other to satisfy hunger below the waistline,' added Ada.

She smiled and handed over the box to Vasiq.

'This also may remind you where we left our conversation in Lucknow,' mocked Ada.

As the day grew a little older, it was time for Ada to head to the airport to get back home. Vasiq requested if he could drive her to the airport. Ada smiled.

They didn't speak a single word from Totteridge to Heathrow.

She walked into the airport. He stood waiting for her to turn back. He was not sure if she would. But she did.

The strangers parted ways. Both had no reason to hold each other back. She wanted to spend a little more time with Vasiq, and he waited for another look of her. None happened.

The river Gomti still flows through the city, and her culture still remains to be loved by Ada of *Lakhnau* while Vasiq once in a while visits with his wife and children but still struggles to identify a reason to visit her!

TELEPHONE

Partha Pratim Sanyal. Better known as Partha in his neighbourhood. Born in late 1960s in posh South Kolkata, Partha had a mixed upbringing of anglicised Bengali culture and Sukumar Roy.

His *MAD* comics graduated to Satyajit Ray's 'Feluda' series. And his *Tintin* graduated to Kafka.

When in school, he read Kafka's short stories and was intrigued by 'Metamorphosis'. Then came the 'Third Eye' by Lobsang Rampa and 'Being and Nothingness' by Satre. He actually understood nothing about the latter, though it was a name to brag about in the young intellectual circuits.

Partha grew up with mixed and conflicting beliefs about the Unknown. His maternal family believed in God, while his paternal family believed that they were God.

The concept of the Unknown always intrigued him, and he never could find a satisfying answer. So the only way out was to experiment. Experiment with different ways and substances to find an answer.

Partha's experiments had their impact on his academics. Factually, on the other hand, he couldn't relate to the lessons taught in class.

This was in 1981, when he failed in his final examination in grade 7. During this time, he had a neighbour called Kaiser, who was about five-odd years older to him and would talk about things that were interesting yet unbelievable.

Kaiser would talk about aliens with green eyes and scales on the body, the entire continent of Eurasia turning upside down with snowfall happening all over India, elephants walking all over Russia, and hypnosis and astral travel!

So when he got his annual report saying, 'Not promoted to Grade 8', Partha went straight to Kaiser and asked him if he knew of any mystic practice that could change his scenario.

He did have a solution. He asked Partha to isolate himself in a dark room and put a candle in front of him.

He was advised to concentrate on the tip of the flame till he could put the candle off with the power of his mind!

Partha was excited in the belief that in an hour or so, he would gain immense power to look at his annual school report and change the status to 'Promoted to Grade 8'. So he ran back home, shut himself in a room, put the lights and fan off, put a candle in front of him, and began to concentrate vigorously on the tip of the flame.

In an hour or so, the flame went off. He was jubilant and felt the energy of his new-found power travel through his entire body. Partha rushed to get up to put on the light so that he could look at his annual school report card and change the status.

He got up and horrifyingly tumbled over something and fell flat on his back. The domestic help ran in and put the lights on. It was Partha's younger brother who was all through hiding under the table. It was he who had sneaked out from under the table and blown the candle off.

Partha was in total frustration that he couldn't evoke the Unknown within. So the next thing was to pray to the God outside . . . And he prayed and prayed till he lost all hope and walked up to his father in the evening to show the report card.

His mother knew of tantric practitioners and believed that they could change the fate of her son's life. She had faith in a *baba* called Kiron. So Partha was taken to Kiron, where they had to buy an entry fee for Rs. 2, which meant that against each coupon, one could only ask one question.

Partha insisted on buying two. His mother was somewhat happy.

They had to stand in a huge queue, and it was not before one hour that Partha's turn came to meet the *baba*. His mother came along for the 'gracious audience'.

Partha had to first give the coupons to the *baba*, who threw them in the holy fire that was lit in front of him. There was an idol of Goddess Kali, and the room was filled with hibiscus flowers. The *baba* wore a red *tilak* on his forehead and sat bare-bodied with tons of *rudraskh* all over him.

Partha's first question was if he could ever become a successful writer. The *baba* looked deep into his eyes and nodded.

Now the second question. Partha asked would he get through if the school allowed a retest. Actually, his mother had applied taking an undertaking that if Partha failed in the retest, he would have no other option but to repeat in Grade 7.

Baba Kiron looked into Partha's eyes and again nodded. He took out a small white piece of cloth that was drenched with *sindoor* and gave it to Partha. The advice that came along was to keep it in the pencil box. It was supposed to do miracles and make Partha clear his retests.

Partha appeared. His mother was sure that her son would be promoted to Grade 8 till she got a call from the school saying that Partha had scored an all-time low of 18 per cent in his aggregate and had no option but to continue in the same grade.

Baba Kiron was not blamed. The conclusion was that some evil spirit had taken over Partha, and he should be taken to a hypnotherapist.

Now the next step was to get an appointment with a hypnotherapist, Dr Swapan Mondal, who was believed to be very powerful with his remedies and could take people back into their past lives; it is popularly known as past life regression therapy and expected to solve all mental and psychological illnesses.

A young Partha, by this time, had learnt the art of rolling up joints and mixing aromatic Prince Henry tobacco to kill the overpowering smell of weed.

So when Partha was taken to the hypnotherapist, he had happily smoked a joint on the terrace and brushed his teeth to avoid any unwanted smell. He was in a state of buzz.

Dr Mondal had him lie down on a reclining chair and put off all lights in the room except for a spot right on top of Partha's head. The doctor asked Partha to close his eyes, take a deep breath, and count backwards slowly from ten to one. Partha obliged, and in a state of buzz, he dozed off.

The doctor was convinced that Partha was in a state of trance and gave commands that were to reach his subconscious to alter his behavioural patterns and habits.

Partha, on realising that he had dozed off, suddenly got up from the reclining chair. The doctor immediately pushed him back and asked him to take a deep breath and count from ten to one as slowly as he could.

A week passed. Partha would spend time following Lobsang Rampa's instructions, trying to concentrate at the tip of his toenail and practise self-hypnosis to enable astral travel. Nothing much happened.

The worst was that he now had taken his repetition in the same grade in his stride and was least bothered. By this time, a close friend, Conchy as he called him, introduced him to The Doors, Cream, Allman Brothers, CCR, and of course The Beatles and Dylan.

Partha knew his lyrics and somehow connected to the sound. He would smoke a joint on the terrace and listen to music all day.

With some savings out of his pocket money, he bought an used pair of torn Levi's jeans from a stall on Sudder Street where the travelling hippies would put up at the

Salvation Army and sell most of their belongings to travel to their next destination.

He would often be heard mumbling, *'Come on baby light my fire'.*

One day he was made to stand outside the classroom as he had forgotten to carry his Civics book.

He had smoked his joint in the morning and was still on a buzz. So when the discipline in-charge of the school, Mr Narshima, was doing his rounds, he found Partha holding his ears and mumbling Bob Dylan's *'The Times They Are A-Changin'.'*

He asked Partha to meet him in his office, and this news spread like wildfire in the school. Everybody knew Partha would be canned and put in the detention room.

Partha went across to Mr Narshima's office and stood quietly outside till he was called in.

Partha was asked to sit. To his utter shock, Mr Narshima took out a cassette, signed it, and gave it to Partha. It was a Woody Guthrie collection!

The neighbourhood also had started noticing Partha's long hair, torn jeans, and unkempt look. The neighbourhood kids were asked to keep away from him.

His aunt and his mother decided to take him back to the hypnotherapist as they knew that one session was not good enough for Partha. The routine this time was the same. The reclining chair. Lights going off. One on top of his head. And the doctor asking him to close his eyes, take a deep breath, and count backwards.

'Now you are in my control . . . You are now five years old. What do you remember . . .?' the doctor continued in a deep voice.

Partha moved his right arm slowly, and before anybody could even understand what was happening, he grabbed the famous hypnotherapist by his testicles.

'Now tell me . . . who is in whose control?' He said that in a deep voice to the doctor. And that was the end!

By this time, it was well declared that Partha was eccentric. And he cared a damn. He still went up to the terrace and smoked his joints and sang his songs.

His relationship with his school had fallen apart with most of his teachers rebuking him at every given opportunity. The final blow came when he was caught by the physical education teacher kissing a senior girl in the toilet. The girl, who was in grade 12, was let off, but Partha was humiliated and thrown out of school.

He couldn't handle this and got hold of the physical education teacher on the streets one day and thrashed the daylights out of him. This attracted a police report, and Partha's father, who otherwise was only concerned with his business, stepped in and used his influences to settle the matter.

Whatever relationship the father and son shared, it ended on this day. It was clear that Partha was a huge point of humiliation for an otherwise prosperous and socially respectable family that had some members in the parliament, some were medical practitioners for royalties in the Middle East, and some were in bureaucracy. Some roads were also named after close ancestors.

A decade passed. Partha still smoked and spent most of his time writing scripts for documentaries and short films that never saw the light of the day. And during the day, he worked for a computer company and would go door-to-door to sell. His salary was enough for him to pay the rent for a one-room set-up in Purbo Putiary on the outskirts of Kolkata and survive, though most of his money would be spent on buying local hooch.

Partha had completely disassociated himself from his family. And truthfully, his family preferred to forget him. With time, he had totally isolated himself.

The cupboard in his 8' by 10' home was filled with only manuscripts. Frustrated as he was unable to share his works with anybody for that matter, he decided to save money and apply for a telephone connection so that he could call his friend, Umesh, in Varanasi, to once in a while share his ideas, scripts, screenplays, poems, and all that he wrote.

Partha had accidentally met Umesh first on a trip to the mountains about eight years back when he was travelling around Yamunotri with a group of *Naga* sadhus. What was he doing there? Well, for the world he was smoking pot, but in actuality, Partha wanted to seek answers for the meaning of the bright white light that he would often see hovering between his eyebrows.

Umesh was a film-maker from Varanasi, who was travelling around in search of subjects. Both met in a village called Kharsali opposite the river in Janakichatti. They went across to visit an ancient temple which was believed to have inscriptions on the wall that even some French curators who had come from the Louvre Museum couldn't decipher.

Both even travelled to Saptarishi Kund, a treacherous 10-km uphill trek from Yamunotri; it is the actual source of the river Yamuna. In the distance was the partly visible peak of Banderpunch.

Partha was convinced that Umesh was the only person who understood him. Umesh had helped Partha understand what the white light was all about, and how it was his own energy that he could see.

So Partha had to get a telephone connection. He had to call Umesh in the privacy of his night when the stray dogs would go to sleep and the thieves would be returning home.

Every night, Partha would call Umesh and discuss a wide range of subjects from mythology to music. He finally had someone who was willing to hear him out.

He, without being challenged, could share that the entire myth of *'Neelkanth'* and *'Samudra Manthan'* was a yogic process that could be performed inside the human body – documented as a story that has travelled from antiquity to us. Partha strongly believed that the image of Goddess Kali was not that of a demon goddess as believed in the West but the representation of a black hole in space. Probably a stargate!

Partha's midnight rendezvous with Umesh carried on for a couple of decades. By this time, Partha was extremely frail and could hardly work. He worked as an operator at a photocopy shop during the day.

He gathered a lot of debt, and one day he had to sell his cupboard. All his manuscripts lay scattered on the floor, and he had no strength to take care of them. Soon he lost his job as the photocopy machine operator and had to gradually sell all the paper on the floor to a *kabariwala*.

Partha had made some ten rupees by selling all his manuscripts that would be either sent to a paper factory to be recycled or made into paper packets. It was hardly enough for him to pay his rent and buy ration but was about enough to buy a bottle of country hooch.

That night, he didn't eat but drank a full bottle and smoked a joint. Without a morsel in his stomach and the pain of losing all his works, he called Umesh, but his telephone number was eternally unreachable that night.

Partha had to call. He had to talk. He had so much to say. But the phone was still unreachable.

The stray dogs calmed down, and the thief went back home. The farmers carried their baskets to the urban markets, and the hot bread straight from the local bakery's oven was also delivered to the nearby convenience stores. The newspapers were being readied to be distributed, and sun was peeping through the eastern horizon.

Partha's empty bottle of hooch lay on the floor. Not far was a clipboard with a manuscript that Partha wrote that night.

A still lifeless body sat relaxed on the broken reclining chair next to a small table. A telephone sat on the table with its receiver in Partha's hand.

When the house owner noticed that there was no movement in the house by 11 a.m., he tried knocking on the door and with the help of neighbours broke it open.

Partha's body was taken away by the police.

A day after Partha's post-mortem, the local police inspector completed the report by writing that the man was an alcoholic and died of a severe cardiac arrest.

Nothing much was found in the room, and no foul play was suspected. Only some writings were here and there that made no sense and a telephone that never had any connection!

The Ballad of Bodhan and Kajri

Adhura Nagar. I had never heard of it ever. I don't think you have too!

Bodhan lived with his newly-wed wife, Kajri, and people of lower caste, otherwise known as *Panchamas*, in the dry wasteland of Adhura Nagar. They could hardly grow anything in the useless stretch of land. So they had to work as labourers doing menial jobs for the upper caste, who lived a kilometre away.

The upper caste had land that could be tilled and produced crops. But the produce was barely enough for their survival. The entire area was barren and dry. It hardly had rainfall.

The dry wasteland where Bodhan and Kajri lived also belonged to the upper caste. He and his community of fourteen families struggled every bit for their survival.

They worked in the fields of the upper caste in exchange of uncooked rice and some greens. The days they couldn't find work, they had to hunt for mouse and mongoose, which they roasted on fire and ate to survive.

There were times when they would sleep without food.

Even though the upper class behaved like zamindars with Bodhan and his people, they too had to struggle hard to survive in the dry barren region of Adhura Nagar.

A dry wide river bed ran in-between the settlements of the two communities.

Both the communities called the river bed Saraswati and believed that the river had gone underground and ran from the high mountains in the north to the sea far away.

They both worshipped Adhura Devi. A small temple was erected by the upper caste by the dry river bed and was out of bounds for Bodhan and his people.

So the lower caste practised rituals to please their gods who they believed fought in the stars long ago. Their blood that fell on earth created humans when mixed with dust.

They would gather hallucinogenic mushrooms from the wild growth alongside the dry river bed, which they consumed to get into a state of trance.

Their houses were made of dry leaves and branches of dead trees that were tied up with ropes that they made with the fibre extracted out of a shrub locally available in the wild growth.

The houses of the upper caste were mostly made of mud and had a thatched roof.

The entire area was so dry that despite having dug as many as seven wells, the upper caste could find water only in one. The well was barricaded with a fence made of dry branches that were tied up together.

No lower-caste person could go even near the trail that led to the well. The adults in Bodhun's village were cautious, as they would be tied to trees for two nights as punishment if they did so by mistake.

Kajri and the women of her community had to travel the entire day to the next village of people of similar fate to fetch water, till they found water after years of struggle.

They erected a well and protected it with all their strength and might.

This didn't go too well with the people of the upper caste. They believed that they only had the right over water in Adhura Nagar. And this was long before the

CEO of an FMCG global company put across the idea of privatisation of water.

First, the heads of the upper-caste community decided that if Bodhan and his community wanted to have rights over the well that they had dug, they would have to send the womenfolk to work as *devdasis* in the temple by the dry river bed.

What this meant was the womenfolk of the lower caste were being forced into ritualistic prostitution.

Bodhun and his community agreed as they had no clue about what they were giving in to till his brother's wife returned home one day, violated by the elders of the upper-caste community.

The village elder of the lower-caste community decided to go and plea for a better solution. He and a few men walked through the path that led to the upper-caste village.

He held an umbrella on his head in the scorching sun; the umbrella was made of leaves gathered from the wild growth alongside the river.

Moment they got closer to the house of the upper-caste village elder, members of the household threw stones at them and repeatedly beat them with sticks till Bodhun's elder brother collapsed, lying unconscious on the ground.

They snatched the umbrella and set it on fire and warned the members of the lower-caste community to refrain from using an umbrella as it was a privilege enjoyed by the upper-caste community only.

Lost, hurt, and bruised they returned home without being able to solve the *devdasi* issue.

Bodhun's brother was attended by the village shaman who lit a bonfire at night and performed a ritual. He made a paste made of wild berries and applied it on his bruises and gave him a mushroom to eat so that the gods could take his pain away.

Next morning, Bodhan went across to the upper-caste village elder's house and begged for an audience. He pleaded that they have access to the water of the well that they had dug and was willing to work for longer hours in the fields and take half the food grain against what they usually got.

But the upper-caste village elder was adamant that the *devdasi* system be continued as it was the best way the lower caste could clean themselves in the service of God.

Bodhun walked back dejected and came home. The next day was the turn of his wife, Kajri, to serve the temple as a *devdasi.*

He didn't speak a single word at home and sat outside his house the entire night. The other members of his community went back to their homes without a single word spoken, dejected, lost, and feeling oppressed.

That night the village was absolutely quiet, and the only sound that could be heard was that of the rats and mice running over dry leaves that lay scattered all around.

At the crack of dawn, Kajri dressed up in her best clothes and walked over to the temple by the dry river bed.

Bodhan followed her and hid himself in the wild growth. Kajri had no clue that her husband had followed her and was keeping a watch.

Kajri sat outside the temple. A couple of hours passed by.

She had carefully kept a dart that she had poisoned with some toxic resin that was found in the wild growth. She kept it hidden under a few dry leaves near the door of the temple. Bodhan was not aware about this.

Another hour and a half further passed by. In the distance was the son of the upper-caste village elder who was walking towards the temple. Bodhan noticed him and sneaked through the wild growth to have a closer look.

The young man in his mid-twenties was drunk. He walked straight up to Kajri and asked her to disrobe. Bodhan was very close and was keeping an eye on the man.

Kajri refused. The man called her a slut and slapped her. Kajri pushed him and rushed towards the temple door. The man grabbed her hand and tried to pull her close.

She kicked him in the groin and ran to take the poisoned dart out of the dry leaves while Bodhan jumped out of the bushes. Before Kajri could pick up the poisoned dart, Bodhan got the young man by his neck and dragged him into the wild growth.

Kajri was shocked to see her husband and stood still.

Bodhan asked her to quickly rush back to the village. She did and was joined by her husband in an hour.

The elders of Bodhan's village were not sure what was happening. They sensed that there was some problem, as Kajri was to come back the next morning. Bodhan too looked tensed.

The sun was going down, and screams could be heard in the distance. They graduated to fire torches coming towards the lower-caste village.

The light and sound got closer and closer. The village stood still. The members of the upper-caste village set every house on flame and tied every male member of Bodhan's community to trees. The women were humiliated.

Only screams could be heard. And the smoke of dry leaves filled the air in the darkness of the night.

The village elder and a few members took Kajri by her hair and pulled her into the bushes. The young boys hid children and young girls behind trees in the wild growth amongst screams and only screams of helplessness.

Kajri lay semi-conscious on the ground.

The upper-caste men untied Bodhan. They pushed him to the ground. He tried to resist but was easily overpowered.

The members of the upper-caste community poured kerosene on him. All screams stopped. Everybody watched in horror. Nobody really knew why they were being subjected to this torture and pain.

The upper-caste village elder lit a matchstick and flicked it at Bodhan. The air echoed with only one scream of Bodhan, who tried to run but fell down to fill the air with the stench of burning human flesh.

Kajri couldn't move and witnessed the horrific death of her husband.

The members of the upper caste pushed Bodhan's lifeless body towards the well.

The next sound that one could hear was that of a huge splash of water. Bodhan's charred body was pushed into the well.

The sun came up. The smell of burnt dry leaves filled the air. Everything was reduced to ashes. Men were still tied to the trees. Humiliated women braved their indignity and walked in the light of the sun to untie their men. Kajri lay still on the ground.

The children started emerging out of the bushes. It was a horrific sight. They all walked towards the well. Bodhan's charred body was floating.

Kajri still lay still on the ground. Hurt and plundered.

Months passed after this terrible incident. The lower-caste village was rebuilt. It was the same routine of torture, rebuke, humiliation, poverty, and forced labour.

Bodhan's community again had to walk the entire day to the next lower-caste village to fetch water. The village shaman performed rituals to drive the evil spirits away. Men still had mushrooms to get into a state of trance, and they still survived on mice and mongoose that they roasted on open fire.

Kajri would sit next to the well. Quiet. Often looking at the waters where her husband's body was thrown. She had become very frail as she would rarely eat.

One day she stopped menstruating. She could feel movements in her womb.

A week passed by.

It was the month of July. There were unexpected rains that splashed over the area. The dark clouds in the sky triggered celebrations in the upper-caste village. The temple bells rang loud.

Kajri walked out of her village. She walked through the path that led to the upper-caste village. Amidst all the celebrations, people didn't notice her.

She walked towards the fencing of the upper-caste well. Crossed it. Kajri stood still looking at the clean waters with drops of rain falling on it.

The village elder's wife had come to fetch some water and noticed Kajari. She raised an alarm. Soon members of the upper-caste community came running with sticks and iron rods, keeping aside all celebrations.

Kajri stood still looking at the waters.

The members came charging towards the well. Kajri looked at the crowd. Smiled. Spit on the ground.

They came closer. And closer. The village elder's wife picked up a stone and threw it at Kajari. It hit her womb.

Kajari stood still while blood that trickled out of her dripped on the ground. The mob was ten feet away.

Before they could lay the first blow on her head, Kajri screamed loudly, looked up at the dark clouds, and jumped into the well.

Everybody suddenly stopped where they were. Their sticks and iron rods fell from their hands. Time stood still for them.

The only sound was that of a thunder in the sky followed by heavy rains with drops falling into the well with Kajri's body floating in it.

The Butcher's Wife and the Monk

Kattapathar is a little distance uphill from Vikasnagar in the plains and about a couple of hours from Dehra Dun, but hardly a distance from Mussoorie via the Yamuna Bridge.

Early morning just before sunrise, strong winds blow in the area, and it is almost impossible to walk. The Yamuna River flows, still in its clear and pristine form.

The area has small villages, some uphill and some by the river. It is a peaceful place with the exception of a legal battle over a temple compound between the priest and a family next door who lived out of harvesting their land.

The temple was run by a *Naga* monk who was a soldier in the Indian National Army. He was born in Haryana when it was still Punjab. Ananda Giri, the head of the temple compound, was a quiet man who spoke Haryanvi and chose not to understand any other language. But late at night, he would tune to BBC World News on his radio.

He was assisted by a monk whom he called Badharey, who came from the foothills of Nepal.

The entire area is full of myths about the Pandavas of *Mahabharat* and how their spirits still possess locals during festivals. Many believe that they are descendants of the Pandavas and the Kauravas.

And besides such myths, another thing that is common at higher altitudes is that there are very small shacks and makeshift temples with ancient idols called *'Bharion Ghati'*.

One such *'Bhairon Ghati'* was en route to Har Ki Doon near Osla. There lived a *Naga* sadhu called Ganga Giri. He was from Chapra in Bihar and had left home at the age of seven when his mother died and his father immediately remarried. Ganga Giri was probably the only monk who was not grumpy in search of *niravana*. He could crack the silliest of jokes and laugh till his voice echoed in the mountains. All his jokes would be on himself.

He was an extremely agile man yet short – about an inch over five. Ganga Giri lived seven months in *Bhairon Ghati,* and the rest of the five months of winter in a year he would live in the temple compound of Ananda Giri.

Both were exactly the opposite poles. If Ananda Giri would sit quietly on the terrace smoking a hookah, Ganga Giri would be running around cleaning the temple compound or going to the woods to gather firewood with Badharey or visit the lawyer in Vikasnagar over the land dispute.

The only time they would spend together would be at around 4 a.m. in the morning. This would be after both had braved the strong winds, taken a bath in absolutely chilled water and cleaned the temple. They would share a cup of tea made on the holy fire or the *Hom Kund.* The only discussion would be if the mules in the higher altitudes were keeping good health.

Many would visit the temple from all across the mountains and the valley of Dehra Dun.

This was in 1997. Ganga Giri had come down from the heights to Ananda Giri's temple the moment the first snow fell.

That year the winter was severe, and the winds were very strong – strong enough to blow a child away.

That year amongst the new visitors was Dimple, who lived in Mussorrie.

Dimple, a forty-two-year-old woman, was trying to walk out on her husband, who owned a prosperous butcher shop in Mussorrie. She was having an extramarital relationship with a young man in his twenties called Pawan.

Pawan was unemployed and was interested in the gifts he got from Dimple rather than on being hit by Cupid's arrow. It was more a lust- and money-driven relationship than anything else.

Dimple wanted to not only walk away from her husband, but she also had an eye on his butcher shop.

The first time they had come, Ganga Giri was in the woods with Badharey to gather some firewood. Ananda Giri was sitting alone under a shade.

The couple walked up to him and sat opposite him, hoping to have a conversation. Ananda Giri was hardly interested in having any conversation.

Dimple, unable to hold back any longer, asked the monk if he could do some black magic by which she could get rid of her husband and get her hands on the butcher shop.

Ananda Giri looked at Dimple. He politely got up, walked to the room where the firewood was kept, picked up a branch, walked back to the couple, and sat down quietly.

Dimple offered him money for any magic that he could do. At this the monk took the stick and chased the couple out of the temple compound.

Pawan was the first one to run out while Dimple could hardly manage with her ninety-odd kilograms of weight.

Ganga Giri returned with firewood, and the day went on as usual. In the evening, like every day, kids from local villages came to have sweets that were routinely offered to the deity.

That evening, Raju, a young orphan from a nearby village, came to meet Ananda Giri. He would come to the temple once or twice a week since his childhood and was loved by all.

He had two cows that were his source of survival, as he would sell the milk from them in the local villages. It was about a month back that a speeding truck had hit both the cows. One died on the spot while the other lost a leg. Since then his business suffered, and his survival was at stake.

Both Ananda Giri and Ganga Giri knew this. Raju was going through a huge amount of stress as he was also paying back some debts that his father had incurred while building their home before his death.

Anyways, days passed. A week passed.

Dimple was convinced that the *Naga* babas at Kattapathar could help her. In-between, she went to Dehra Dun to see a Bengali tantric who had given her a few mustard seeds that she was supposed to hide in her husband's pillow. This would make her husband go insane, and she could then gradually take over his business and carry on with her relationship with Pawan.

Needless to say, nothing happened, and the Bengali tantric too disappeared with some Rs. 20,000 that he had charged for the magic.

So Dimple and Pawan went back to Kattapathar, hoping to convince one of the Naga babas to help her in her game plan.

It was early morning. Ganga Giri was watering the fields when the couple arrived. They requested for an audience, and the monk asked them to wait till he finished his job. They did.

When Ganga Giri heard the reason that was behind their coming all the way from Mussoorie, he asked them to leave. Dimple fell on his feet and begged for some magic that could turn the events of her life in the direction that she wanted.

Ganga Giri, unable to be rude, told the couple that he would give it a thought later. Pawan and Dimple left with some hope.

Again days passed. A week passed. A fortnight passed.

The couple returned. This time Ananda Giri saw them enter the temple compound. He sat quietly and kept a watch while smoking his hookah.

They sat in front of the temple, waiting to be called by either Ananda Giri or Ganga Giri.

Ganga Giri, as usual, was out with Badharey for some firewood. Winter had set in. The need to keep the fire alive and strong was critical.

Pawan and Dimple had waited for over two hours when they saw Ganga Giri walk in with a huge pile of firewood on his back. He walked straight past them and dumped the firewood in the room.

He walked out and started cleaning the temple. Dimple went up to Ganga Giri and asked him if he was willing to help. The monk was tired and irritated. He sternly asked them to leave and not return ever again.

Dimple this time was firm that she wouldn't go empty-handed. She begged the monk and offered him money.

Ganga Giri threw the broom, walked up to Dimple and asked if she knew the amount of money required to perform such magic.

He then walked to the holy fire and sat. The couple followed and sat opposite him.

'Fifty thousand!' said Ganga Giri. Dimple was more than willing to spend the money to get rid of her husband and get her hands on the butcher shop.

Ganga Giri asked them to wait. He walked inside the temple and came back. He dramatically threw something into the fire that made the flame go up by three feet, and the area was filled with smoke and stench.

Dimple got scared and held Pawan's hand, which had already started sweating. Again, Ganga Giri threw something in the fire, and the same phenomenon was repeated.

Ganga Giri theatrically sat right in front of them. There was a huge amount of drama happening while Ananda Giri kept on smoking his hookah.

The place was filled with stench of burning human flesh. There was smoke all over, but the fire finally settled down. Dimple and Pawan were daring the experience as the greed of taking over the butcher shop was burning them from inside!

Ganga Giri looked at them with big red eyes and asked Dimple if she could smell human flesh burning. She was trebling. She said she could.

He looked at Pawan and asked them to come back early next morning with the money. While they were going out, confused and yet hopeful, Ganga Giri told them that the stench was that of Dimple's husband's flesh burning from inside, and soon he would turn insane.

The couple was convinced and went back happy.

The next morning, they came back with the money. Ganga Giri, as usual, was out with Badharey for firewood. Dimple couldn't wait and handed over a packet with the money to Ganga Giri the moment he returned from the nearby woods.

Ganga Giri took the money and asked them to leave. But before sending them off, he gave Dimple some dry leaves and asked her to chew them every morning before breakfast and abstain from having sex with Pawan.

This was to turn her husband insane within a fortnight. He warned that if she failed to follow the process, all his efforts would fall flat.

Dimple religiously followed the routine. Pawan started counting days in anticipation. Days passed.

Ananda Giri was extremely angry with Ganga Giri over the incident and stopped talking about mules with him in the early dawn before sunrise.

Days passed.

Raju came to meet Ananda Giri and cried as he was unable to manage the crisis in his life. The sun was going down. The local kids came in, as usual, for the sweets. 'Bhadharey' cleaned up the temple before the daily distribution.

Raju stood with them with wet eyes and an uncertain future. The kids were becoming restless. It was gradually getting dark, and they all had to go a long way back home.

Ganga Giri playfully distributed the sweets while cracking silly jokes with the kids. He came to Raju and stopped. He looked into his eyes and gave him sweets and a packet.

Raju had the sweets and opened the packet to see plenty of money in it. He walked up to Ganga Giri, confused. The monk told him that it contained Rs. 50,000. That was enough to buy two cows and settle his life once again with one promise that Raju would take care of the ailing cow till she died.

The young lad fell at Ganga Giri's feet and cried like a child. In the distance the sun went down the horizon with Ananda Giri watching the whole episode from a distance and smoking his hookah.

Raju went back home cutting through the darkness of the night. Ganga Giri joined Badharey and made some tea on the holy fire or the *Hom Kund*.

While having his tea, he cracked jokes on himself and told Badharey that if he could change anybody's life, he wouldn't be shuttling like a ping-pong ball to run away from the extreme winter and snow that engulfs *Bhairon Ghati*.

When Badharey asked what if the couple came back for their money, Ganga Giri laughed out loud. He told Badharey that the stench of human flesh that came out of the fire was due to the effect of a handful of rubber bands that he threw in along with a resin that comes from a plant in the mountains that helps fire to grow. When thrown in, the fire jumps into a flame and then settles down to last longer with minimal firewood in it.

And with a wink, he added that the dry leaves that he had given Dimple was a natural aphrodisiac that was easily available in mountain forests.

Ganga Giri laughed his heart out, and it echoed through the mountains while the children went off to sleep in an otherwise peaceful place in the lap of the Himalayas.

The Telescope

Mr Ashutosh Dash, originally from Bhuwaneshwar, worked all his life in Hyderabad as a human resource professional in the information technology sector. His wife, Mitali, was a homemaker who had a habit of standing almost all day in her first-floor balcony and keeping herself updated with neighbourhood gossip.

People in her locality had to put up heavy curtains to keep their homes protected from the probing eyes of Mitali. Dinner table conversation at the Dashses would be about Swathi's affair with Ganesh or Tabassum not being able to conceive or how Mr Venkatesh Swamy had a soft corner for the domestic help, and that Suresh and family had gone out to *Paradise* for dinner.

Ashutosh never really objected to such intrusive behaviour of his wife, instead he also participated in neighbourhood gossip when back home. So it's needless to say that their son Neil grew up in an atmosphere where probing was his second nature. He had the habit of going up to the terrace in the evenings to find an opportunity to look into neighbourhood bedrooms.

Ashutosh had applied for the job of Head – Learning and Development – with a blue chip company in Gurgaon. So when he got the job, he chose to move into a nice apartment in a condominium near the Golf Course since his office in Cyber City was ten minutes away from home.

Neil got admission in a school in the vicinity. It took them about a month to settle down in the new apartment, though adapting to Gurgaon lifestyle became a major issue with the family as it was culturally so different from Hyderabad.

But in a few months, the Dash family switched their lifestyle to sporting top-end brands and sometimes fakes bought from their trip to Bangkok. Ashutosh, who always used a regular pen, upgraded to a Mont Blanc, while his wife, Mitali, soon joined a kitty party circuit where she could satisfy her passion for neighbourhood gossip.

Neil, on the other hand, took too much of time to make friends in Gurgaon. He got tired of surfing on Internet and reading his new-found interest, *The Simpsons.*

And the design of the condominium was such that he couldn't go up to the terrace. But he could see some glass panes of a few living rooms across his building.

So one day when Ashutosh returned home from work, Neil shared his interest about the night sky and constellations with his father.

Not long after that Ashutosh got his son a simple telescope on a rusty stand to explore his interest in the night sky. Neil, with the help of his father, positioned the telescope in their balcony that overlooked an empty stretch of land.

And that was it!

Neil would pull all curtains and lock his room on the pretext of studying intensely while his parents discussed all that was happening under the sky in the condominium.

Neil would move his telescope from the balcony and place it at his window overlooking the building across, concealed by the curtains and the darkness of his room.

He would aim at the building across, but all his telescope could do was focus into three apartments on three respective floors opposite his window. This was largely because of the rusty ball bearing on the stand that restricted too much of movement.

Straight opposite his window was the apartment of the Kumars. Prakash Kumar was from Darbhanga in Bihar, having changed his name from Gupta to Kumar.

He was a simple man who had worked his way up from modest upbringing and was the national head of a leading social media company in India.

Despite his success, both socially and financially, he remained a very modest man. He preferred to use a hatchback, unlike his colleagues and his wife who drove their Audis and Beamers.

His wife, Akriti, was a Sindhi from Chandigarh whose father was a leading diamond merchant. She knew the art of socialising and being the focal point of any party without being cerebral.

Akriti was very often covered in page threes of leading dailies, as she was visible at various events from a fashion designer's launch of spring collection to the launch of a modelling school. But what she did for a living was more a mystery as she claimed that she was a leading hairdresser, and no one had any idea where her salon was!

Neil could easily set his eyes inside their apartment with his intrusive tool. Prakash Kumar usually came back from work at around 7 p.m. and sat on the sofa right across the focal point of Neil's telescope. He would chat with his five-year-old daughter for a while and then get up to fix a drink and park himself back on the same place and play games with his little one.

By this time, the domestic help would get him something to eat while Akriti would be gearing up to go out. Dinner at home for her would be if she was unwell or if there was a social gathering at her place.

With a twenty-degree tilt upwards across Neil's window, he could look into the apartment of an artist by the name of Sailesh Mahato. Mahato came to North India from a small village in Purulia district in West Bengal to study in a university in New Delhi, where he completed his masters in fine arts in the 1980s.

Mahato's easel could be clearly seen through the all-intrusive telescope of Neil especially because of the bright lighting of the room. The aging artist was a rage amongst the nouveau riche class who liked to decorate their walls with Mahato's paintings that would go with the decor of their rooms. Many a times, the artist would get commissioned work where he had to paint with colours that matched with the shades of his clients' furniture.

Mahato for many years worked as an art teacher in a few schools in New Delhi and Gurgaon. His works never sold as he lacked the skill to build professional relationship with curators. Besides, he carried a subtle arrogance, which was detrimental to his business.

It was only recently when Mahato found a friend in an Irish girl who had a large client base in North India that things started changing for him. She worked on Mahato's looks from a simple kurta-clad artist with oiled hair to artificial dreadlocks and a flowing beard. She spent money and engaged a PR agency that in turn got the artist a good amount of print and electronic media visibility. Now after this, selling Mahato's works at a steep price, after her commission, was not really tough.

Soon, Mahato was the centre of attraction in condominium parties, and his works sold well enough for him to afford an apartment in the heart of Gurgaon. But the artist from Purulia in him was living in immense pain of compromising with his artistic and creative capabilities.

With another twenty-degree tilt downwards from Neil's window, Neil could observe the apartment where lived an elderly couple, Mr and Mrs Rajan, whose son was in Singapore with his family. The lonely couple found engagement in conversations with each other and reading books. The elderly man mostly spent his time on a rolling easy chair, reading classical literature.

One day in the summers of North India, Neil closed his room and pulled the curtains. He focused his telescope at the Kumars' at a zero-degree tilt.

It was 8 p.m., and the room was very dimly lit. Prakash Kumar was not on the sofa, but his daughter lay on it with her legs pulled inwards, almost in a fetal position. The child seemed to be crying while the domestic help sat on the floor consoling the child.

Well, Neil was not interested in this and shifted his focus on Mahato's floor. Coincidently, Mahato was painting a street urchin, cramped up in a fetal position and crying next to a garbage bin. But the colours were too bright and loud to depict the state of mind of the child. It almost seemed like the walls of a Hindi soap opera set with bright colours thrown in to match the costumes of the actors.

Neil again tilted his telescope to the Kumars. The child still lay on the sofa. Akriti walked out of a room in her boots and hemp skirt. She lit a cigarette and tossed the child's hair and walked out with the domestic help, locking the door.

Nothing interesting for Neil. So he reluctantly tilted towards the Rajans. The elderly man was reading *Shakuntalam,* and at a distance his wife had a Khalil Gibran in hand. Occasionally, the elderly couple took turns to read out parts from their books.

For a few days, Prakash couldn't be seen. And the rest of the routine was almost the same – the little girl crying, and the domestic help consoling her while Akriti would walk out for her late-night social gatherings.

One evening, when Neil tilted his telescope to Mahato's window, he saw the artist in a heated argument with the Irish girl. The girl grabbed Mahato's linseed oil bottle and threw it on his canvas. Then she grabbed his flat brush and smudged his painting while Mahato desperately tried pulling her back. The girl pointed her finger aggressively at the artist and seemed to threaten him. She rushed out and slammed the door on his face.

The worried and visibly angry artist walked back to his easel and lit a cigarette and stood still in front of the canvas.

It was over a week, and Prakash hadn't returned. He had to travel extensively to Philippines and parts of Africa and was travelling to set up new low-cost back-end offices.

Neil kept his probe alive and focused his telescope on the elderly couple. They both had a copy of *Comedy of Errors,* and it seemed they were reading out parts and enacting roles while laughing their hearts out. Mr Rajan, at one point, got up and kept his book on his easy chair. He walked up to Mrs Rajan and went down on his knees. He took a rose out of the vase and gave it to her. The elderly lady almost seemed to blush and gave her husband a smile.

Neil was not much interested in the romance of an aging couple. So he quickly tilted the telescope towards Prakash's apartment. The child was not on the sofa. The domestic help was not there, but a tanned thin man sat with a glass of whisky on the centre table in front of him and a cell phone in his hand. He seemed to be waiting for somebody while enjoying his whisky and doing something on his phone. In all likelihood, he was checking his mails or networking on social media.

It was about 9.30 p.m. Neil had his dinner and got back to the telescope. He was curious about what the artist was doing. The easel stood where it was. The same smudged canvas rested on it. Mahato had a brush in his hand and was painting a bright red *tika* that was dripping like fresh blood on the canvas. He then painted two eyes on both sides in white and a round nose pin to depict the nose.

At this, the artist walked towards the door. Akriti walked in with the dark thin man who was in her living room a while back. They all walked towards the easel and stood there for a while. Mahato seemed to explain something extensively while the couple studied the smudged painting from all sides.

The tanned thin man looked at his watch, shook his head, and left with Akriti.

Neil, before going off to sleep, tilted his telescope towards the Rajans. Much to his shock, the couple seemed to be elegantly dancing the waltz with Mr Rajan looking into his wife's eyes with affection.

Days passed, and Prakash was still not back. It was about 8 p.m. The little girl lay on the sofa sobbing with the domestic help consoling her. Akriti was behind the sofa fixing up something on the wall. She was in her formals and walked towards the door and opened it. There stood the tanned thin man; the domestic help picked up the child and went inside.

Akriti playfully pulled the man inside and both sat very close on the sofa. She ran her long nails through his curly hair. Now Neil had something of interest happening after such a long wait. The couple kissed and was soon in a compromising position.

At the back of the sofa was a new painting on the wall. It was a street urchin crying in a fetal position near a garbage dump with bright colours that almost matched the colours of Akriti's living room.

The lights went off, and now things were left to Neil's imagination.

Neil was back at the telescope after half an hour. The lights were still off. So he titled it towards Mahato's apartment.

The aging artist seemed wild. Everything in his room was scattered. He pulled down everything from his walls and threw them on the floor. He also threw the smudged painting with eyes, *tika,* and nose pin. He then took a knife and slit the stretched canvas into pieces. Mahato even picked up his easel and hit it repeatedly on the floor till it broke into pieces.

At this, the lights at the Kumars, which was just the floor down, were lit.

Mahato took all his paints and started throwing them all over his walls and ceiling with them dripping down like rain. While he was doing this, the crimson red paint fell on him. He seemed to be hurt and bleeding profusely.

Neil was taken aback. He was not sure about what was happening. Mahato went on for half an hour till he sank on his knees on the floor and seemed to be crying.

His room looked like a painting that he had suppressed for years now. The colours were still fresh and dripping. Mahato got up. He cleared his floor of the damaged canvas and the easel. Mopped it. Cleaned it with turpentine oil. Wiped his face with a cloth and sat in the middle of the floor.

He had tears rolling down his cheeks and had a smile on his face. A smile that seemed full of contentment. Mahato looked happy.

Days passed.

Prakash was back. He returned at 7 p.m. and spent a good two hours playing with the child and laughing and sharing jokes. Both father and daughter giggled and rolled on the floor, playing pranks.

The domestic help with a smile on her face came with some titbits for Prakash, which all of them sat on the floor and had.

Neil focused the telescope down at the Rajans. The lady was sitting on the easy chair. She had no book in her hand and sat with a blank look while the chair swayed forwards and backwards.

He tried moving the telescope looking for the elderly man but stopped at a photograph of his on the wall with a fresh garland on it and *agarbatti*s on a small stand in front. The gentleman in the photo seemed to be smiling and looking affectionately at his wife.

Neil became sad and went off to sleep.

A few days passed, and he hadn't peeped into anybody's house.

It was raining. His urge to intrude in the privacy of others was so deep-rooted in his DNA coding that Neil focused his telescope at the Rajans.

The apartment seemed empty. His focus went to something unusual where the easy chair was.

New people had moved in. The apartment was being set up for the new family.

There stood a boy where the easy chair was. He was looking through a telescope, and Neil's apartment seemed to be in focus!

STARGATE AT SONAGACHI

Abridged version

Jeetu Halder, a young man from Barrackpore, worked in a sari shop in Central Kolkata.

Jeetu had heard about the infamous red-light district of Kolkata called *Sonagachi* from fellow passengers of the 6.45 a.m. local train, which he would take regularly.

One day after work, Jeetu decided to visit the area. He walked through a tunnel of women waiting to be sold on both sides of the street like vegetables. Some touched him. Some winked at him.

He was keen but scared with not much money in his pocket. Jeetu stopped at a hole in the wall selling cigarettes and paan. From the shopkeeper he gathered that Doma was the best he could afford. She was on the top floor of *Nepali Kuthi*.

The curious signage in front of a door right next to the staircase of *Nepali Kuthi* did astonish him a bit. It read that it was the 'private household of a respectable family'.

Still a little unsure, Jeetu walked up to the terrace and asked for Doma. Quick negotiations took place, and he was sent to the corner room. At the door stood a fair good-looking girl with Mongoloid features. Her lips were red with the paan that she was chewing.

Jeetu soon became a regular visitor of *Nepali Kuthi,* and on most occasions he would spend time talking to Doma. Once, on her birthday, he gifted her *Paradise Scent for Girls* that he had bought from a vendor on the Barrackpore – Sealdah local train.

Once, Jeetu came to meet Doma and didn't go back home. And there was no news of him either for over a couple of days. His new mobile was also 'out of reach'.

The police got into action and started their investigation. They went to the shop where Jeetu worked and finally landed in *Nepali Kuthi* to interrogate Doma.

The efforts of the cops to find out if Jeetu had any altercation with the local pimps and goons resulted in no clue as well. So they decided to investigate around the bus stoppage area at the entry of *Sonagachi.*

While they were desperately trying to get some clue, they found an old beggar sleeping on the sidewalk about fifteen feet away.

The cops gave the old man a cigarette and asked if he had seen anything unusual in the past week at the bus stoppage. They showed a photograph of Jeetu Halder to the old man.

The old man screamed, 'Ghost!'

There was a slight mist, and the temperature had fallen down by a couple of degrees – the usual nip in the air before the pujas in Kolkata.

Jeetu was last seen at the bus stoppage. The beggar had noticed something unusual. There was a green haze around Jeetu that grew heavier. It covered everything around the young salesman.

Gradually the haze cleared a bit, and there was nothing. He had disappeared right in front of the eyes of the old beggar.

Jeetu was sucked into a tunnel and was lifted in mid-air. He seemed to travel at a very high speed through the tunnel in a spiral motion. All around him appeared lights.

There were dendrite-like colourful objects interconnected with each other floating all over. There were thunders that released sparks and lightning. It was getting colder and colder. The speed got faster and faster till suddenly everything stopped. Jeetu was floating in mid-air surrounded by a variety of lights that looked like the aurora borealis.

Jeetu Halder was convinced that he was dead, and his soul was travelling out of his body and the world.

The green haze cleared up. The spectacular light show stopped. It was dawn. The sun lazily came out in the eastern horizon. Birds flew out of their nests.

Jeetu was no more floating. No dendrite-like things. No aurora borealis. He was standing at the bus stoppage and was alive.

At a close distance, Jeetu noticed a large group of weird-looking people with weapons that looked straight out of a Hollywood sci-fi movie. Suddenly, on getting a little closer, they pushed Jeetu in the centre and created a couple of rings around him.

There was a large hovercraft over his head that shot a beam of light that fell directly on him. Now poor Jeetu had no clue about what was happening and passed out!

When Jeetu gained consciousness, he noticed that human-like creatures who were short with very big foreheads without any eyebrows or eyelashes had surrounded him.

They had parietal eyes. Such eyes are photoreceptive and are associated with the pineal gland. It regulates circadian rhythmicity and hormone production for thermoregulation. They also had no hair on their bodies and wore no clothes.

In simple terms, the creatures were human-like with eyes like a reptile. Their eyes were connected with a part of their brain that had the pineal gland. The hormone secreted from their pineal glands opened unknown dimensions of their brains, making them psychic.

Such hormones also balanced and controlled the rhythm in their bodies, which defined and let them control various cycles of time, besides generating a series of hormonal reactions that also let the beings control the body temperature, which was conducive to their environment.

He tried getting up when one of the creatures requested him to lie down and rest for a while. Jeetu was amazed to notice that he could hear the voice, but the creature hadn't spoken a single word. His lips, which were just a slit, didn't move, nor did it open its mouth to speak.

Jeetu could hear that he was missing for the past couple of hours and was on an official trip when rescued by the royal guards from the streets on earth. Jeetu asked him how without speaking they were talking to each other.

The creature with pineal eyes informed him that they had stopped speaking aeons ago. Only people on earth, who live 355,600 years back in time, still speak in spoken languages.

Jeetu had enough of this and wanted to get back home. His love for Doma was tearing the hymen of his patience. At this point, in walked another creature. He came up to Jeetu and looked into his eyes. He transmitted information, without using any sensory channel, that some virus that they believed was eradicated 300,000 years back had affected Jeetu's mind.

This virus trapped the mind into believing the hologram that they lived in to be real. It also triggered emotions that led to reproduction of the same kind – which would mean the cycle of life and death.

The creature touched Jeetu's forehead, and he immediately fell motionless on the bed. They put some patches on his forehead, and like litmus paper, they changed colour.

Jeetu got up with no memory of his family, hometown, the sari shop, Doma, or anything for that matter. He even forgot his name.

The human-like creatures with reptilian eyes left him alone in the room.

When he looked out of his window, he saw that there was no land. Everything was floating on what looked like gas. Looking at the sky, he noticed something like the aurora borealis all over. There was no sun.

He remembered that his name was Sirus X11, and he knew who he was. He also had pineal eyes.

Sirus X11 teleported himself to a place that was the seat of governance and justice. Creatures with reptilian eyes had been waiting for him. Nobody wore any clothes and had no reproductive organs. Nobody spoke a single word to communicate; yet they all were having conversations with each other.

Sirus X11 was the chief of prisons and was also holding the highest seat of judiciary. Creatures had assembled at the court of justice for the trial of two who had dared to live together as family and dared to love each other. It was a crime as the virus was eradicated and declared illegal some 300,000 years back.

Sirus X11 gave them their sentence.

The *criminals* had to be erased of all memories, almost like formatting our computers. Their bodies were to be fossilised and kept in test tubes made of crystal.

DNA extracted out of their bodies were teleported through intergalactic cross-dimensional star gates to earth, where they would be born as humans to serve their sentence. They would be deprived of all knowledge and would spend most of their lives trying to figure out who they actually are.

They would be born out of another human's body and reproduce and finally die to be recycled in the same system till they put effort to activate their dormant brain cells by processes that were laid out in the various prison journals for rehabilitation. All such journals had a snakehead, depicting the pineal eye and its effects, as a common logo.

The only way back home was knowledge that lay hidden in the dormant part of their brains.

By this time on earth, Jeetu's family and the police released his photographs in print media in the missing person sections while some sleazy magazines published stories about a salesman disappearing from a brothel while making love.

Sirus X11 remembered how his race had co-created the first life on Earth with microbes hidden in astral boulders that carried water. They fired such meteorites that hit the surface, resulting in huge explosions that made the oceans, land, trees, and the first unicellular life on earth. The first human was created by injecting DNA samples collected from their own bodies into life forms on earth.

First, a male was created. The DNA was extracted from his ribs, and after some experiments, a female was produced. That triggered the beginning of mankind. When, after the initial attempts, the experiments did not yield the desired results, genetic engineering was carried out by tweaking things at the core level.

When there was an overflow of prisoners on earth, Sirus X11 would manipulate the weather and create tsunamis, flash floods, and volcanic eruptions.

Sirus X11 was always apprehensive of rebellion amongst prisoners and their offspring on earth. He knew that the weakness of mankind was lack of information and knowledge. He strategised to use the fear of unknown against them to oppress rebellion before it could put its head up.

Sirus X11's propagandas have resulted in so many religions and sects within them on earth that mankind still spends most of its time either fighting one another over beliefs or in its struggle to exist.

Though the various journals of Sirus X11's prison are meant for salvation of mankind, the trick lies in-between the lines.

As mentioned in all journals, one of the most fundamental ways of tapping dormant cells of the brain for knowledge and salvation is by using the five vibrations of the five fundamental elements that are prevalent on earth – earth, water, fire, wind, and space.

Each element has its own vibration, and when these vibrations are used effectively, it balances the discrepancies of nature within man and on earth.

The five vibrations are *Na, Mah, Si* (pronounced *Shi*), *Vah, and Yah.*

Sirus X11 has played with human memory and beliefs so much that the five vibrations that have the power of opening the dormant brain cells of mankind are now mispronounced with hardly any impact as desired.

Sirus X11 very carefully has spread the information about left and right brains but kept the understanding of the key element of the brain away from mankind.

His agents have spread the information through chosen scientists and practitioners, keeping mankind in dark about the strength and the potential of the mid brain.

The mid-brain secretes a chemical which, when triggered, makes man naturally intoxicated while opening the dormant cells of the brains. And the more it happens, more and more does man have access to all the information and knowledge that they are deprived of.

And mankind follows its natural instinct for this need to be in a state of intoxication or high by smoking marijuana or hashish, drinking alcohol, sniffing chemicals, etc., though the effect of cannabis is believed to be the closest to the deprived sensation.

Sirus X11 knew that if man can trigger this chemical reaction in their brains, they would gradually start coming back from prison earth and would create a situation of population influx in his civilisation.

But then someone on earth did mention that every action has an equal an opposite reaction. Sirus X11 too had to face his fate and be accountable for his actions.

A shower of huge comets that were creating havoc in space passed so close to the gaseous body of Sirius that it triggered a chemical reaction. The result was that the entire body of light-emitting gas was engulfed in flames. It soon was a huge ball of fire, destroying every little thing on it.

This caused the annihilation of Sirus X11's civilisation. Sirus X11 was burnt to ashes. No advanced technology could save the disaster.

Sirus X11 was not very sure about what was happening as it all happened so soon and so fast. He suddenly found himself travelling at a very high speed in spiral motion through a huge tunnel. There were dendrite-like things interconnected with each other floating in the zero-gravity tunnel.

There were a variety of lights all around. There were sparks and lightning. The spectacular display of light had so many fluorescent shades of all possible colours. Sirus X11 now knew what was happening.

Suddenly everything stopped. Sirus X11 was floating in mid-air. There was no light. No tunnel. No spark. No lightning.

It was late evening. There was a little nip in the air. He stood some fifteen feet away from the bus stoppage. Jeetu wanted to call his home. But he couldn't find his cell phone.

He rushed to *Nepali Kuthi*. Jeetu had to tell Doma that he wanted to marry her. He rushed up the dark staircase.

There was a little crowd in front of the corner room. He tried pushing his way through. A body lay on the ground covered with a white sheet. He went closer. And closer.

There lay a very old woman with Mongoloid features. She was dead. People picked up the body and started walking down the dark staircase. There was silence.

Jeetu was not much interested in the dead body being taken way. He was looking for Doma.

There stood a beautiful young girl with Mongoloid eyes at the doorstep, waiting for customers. Jeetu enquired about Doma.

She winked and said, 'I am Doma.'

Jeetu Halder ran as fast as he could down the staircase. People were still climbing down with the body of the old frail woman. Her lips were still red with paan that she must have chewed moments before she died.

The air was filled with drums of celebrations in the distance. It was the last day of Durga Puja. Idols were being taken to the Ganges to be immersed in the river.

The body was put inside a hearse. The funeral coach struggled to find its way through the endless processions of idols while Jeetu stood motionless.

He could hear somebody chanting *'Namo Shivaya.'* The sound came from the 'private household of a respectable family'.

The Guilt

Aunty Sharon would knit a woollen garment for Frankie while Uncle Jeremiah would smoke a '*buckshot*' on his easy chair. In the background would play 'I Am a Railroad Bum' by Jim Reeves on the gramophone while Sandra would be chopping vegetables and peeling potatoes for the shepherd's pie for dinner while the beef mince cooked on the stove.

Frankie was a stray dog whom Uncle Jeremiah, who was popularly known as Uncle Jerry, got home on a Christmas night.

Jeremiah Gardener and his family lived on the mezzanine floor of a four-storeyed building which had common toilets. Mornings would be chaotic with the boys pushing each other, while the ladies would be respectfully given room first.

'Bugger, I got here first. I damn left the *mugga* here . . . and you man pushed it aside when I went to get a matchbox to light my *'buckshot'* . . . damn you!'

'Move your brown arse back and behave like an Anglo, man!'

'We never spoke ever like this in Nagpore. The boys speak like Indians.'

'Cut your shit out, Johny. I can't hold it any more.'

This was the regular routine from 5.30 a.m. to 9 a.m. in the four-storeyed building where the Gardeners, the Suarezes, the Browns, the Emmanuels, the D'Costas, and the McMillan's lived.

Uncle Jerry worked in the Indian Railways. He was in charge of catering on a north-bound train and had retired.

His son, Shaun Gardener, lived in Sydney and worked as a construction supervisor, and every month he sent some money home. Aunty Sharon worked as a matron in a Protestant school in the locality. Sandra, a young pretty lady, worked in an export company as a receptionist.

Though they lived in a one-room outfit, money was never in abundance; also, never was there a crisis.

Shaun was saving to buy a two-room apartment as he was planning to marry on his next trip to India. Sandra too was saving to migrate to Northern Ireland.

Her maternal uncle, Stan Beechem, who lived in Newry, had promised her a job.

Uncle Jerry's pension and Aunty Sharon's salary were good enough for them to live happily.

Stan Beechem and family had migrated two decades back and detached themselves from their Indian roots. His father worked as a general manager in the Western Railways and left India the moment he retired.

Sundays were very important for two reasons: one, the Mass at the church, and second, the lunch at home.

Uncle Jerry wore his black suit even on a summer morning while Aunty Sharon took out her best floral frock. Sandra wore her best skirt with a thick black leather belt around the waist and wore stilettoes. The ladies wore a white lace headdress while Uncle Jerry always donned his classic red Tartan Scottish flat cap.

Joesph D'Costa's son Alfred had a soft corner for Sandra. Sunday Mass was the best time he could spend a little time with her after the prayer.

Alfred's proposal for marriage was rejected both by Uncle Joseph and Uncle Jerry since he didn't have a steady job. And moreover, the attention was fine with Sandra, but she had no intentions of marrying in India.

The young boys of the building gathered at the entry of the dark and wide wooden staircase in the evenings. They would strum the guitar and sing songs by Neil

Diamond, Cliff Richard, and Glen Campbell while most had a pompadour haircut that got popular in the 1950s.

A little fling and lip-locking behind the staircase was a regular scene with the young well-dressed boys and the young fashionable girls who lived in the building.

Most Sundays, Uncle Jerry would unleash his expert cooking skills. It was a general tradition to share a bowl of what cooked in the house with the immediate neighbour. So on Sundays, the entire building would be having a party over railway mutton curry, chicken jaalfrezi, trotter soup, ball curry, yellow rice, beef roast, and sausage curry, which would be followed by Aunty Brigitte's plum cake in the evening that she would distribute amongst all.

The men, who loved their spirits, gathered in the evening at Uncle Jerry's and would pull in money to buy some dark rum. Aunty Sharon would make dry beef liver fry.

The men would strum their guitars and sing songs by Kingston Trio, Louis Armstrong, and Elvis Presley, and once in a while, the ladies joined in with 'Itsy Bitsy Teenie Weenie Yellow Polka Dot Bikini' or some songs by Doris Day while the ole men blushed.

Some of them would often step out of the mezzanine floor of Uncle Jerry's to do their twist on the landing of the staircase, while the young ones gathered at Aunty

Brigitte's on the top floor and danced to 'Footloose' and the 'Heat Is On'.

They never had to go out of their building to party on a Sunday. It was a happy neighbourhood that would again get up in the morning to struggle for their turn to relieve themselves.

Life was a big happy place for all of them.

During the day, most went out for work. Uncle Jerry started getting bored of his retired life with reading the daily and listening to the gramophone.

So he found a friend who helped him to get a job as a supervisor in a warehouse. It was on a summer afternoon that he had a severe cardiac attack at work and was rushed to a nearby government hospital.

After three days of struggle, Uncle Jerry passed away even before he could be put on the ventilator.

Shaun couldn't get a leave and had to give up his job to immediately return to India to be with his family and to do the rites.

Within forty days of mourning, there was another setback for the Gardeners. Aunty Sharon suffered a stroke while taking a wash and died.

The entire building was in a state of severe shock. The music and the parties stopped. Everybody was in a state of mourning.

Shaun was going through a family crisis, and on top of it, he had an employment issue. He couldn't leave his young sister alone and head back to Australia with another job. As if this was not good enough, Sandra lost her job for not being able to cope up with the new work pressure; the emotional turmoil that she was going through had started taking its toll.

Suddenly within a span of two months, everything changed at the Gardeners'. Shaun decided to put all his savings in a small two-room apartment on the outskirts of the city before the money was consumed in daily expenses.

He paid in full for an apartment and decided to shift with his sister and postpone his marriage plans till he found a job. By this time, he was left with very little money though Sandra had her savings intact, which she had set aside to migrate to Ireland.

Came a day when the young Gardeners moved out of the warmth of a 125-year-old heritage building and the neighbourhood where they had grown up, in search of a new life.

A couple of months passed. One day, the young Gardener received a registered mail from a lawyer saying that a property agent had cheated the original owner of the property and the apartment was illegally sold to Shaun. The sky fell on him.

Before he could react, he found himself in a legal mess and realised that the apartment had been sold to five buyers. The court sent an eviction notice, and Shaun and his sister were asked to vacate the place.

They didn't have an option and kept all belongings in a warehouse close to their old home where the senior Emmanuel worked and found shelter at the D'Costas.

A couple of weeks passed. Stan Beechem was on a visit to India on a business trip. When Sandra got to know of this, she kept the information away from Shaun and met her uncle with dreams of migrating to Ireland.

The uncle was fond of his young niece and soon agreed to help Sandra to migrate out of India.

Shaun had no clue and was of the idea that Sandra was looking for a job. He went helter-skelter looking for work for himself, but it seemed that the dark clouds were still looming over the Gardeners.

Soon, Shaun's last bit of saving was consumed, and he still had no job. The D'Costas provided the young brother and sister with all that they could. Shaun had no idea what was cooking behind him, and one night, Sandra came back home to inform that her visa was done and she was flying back with Uncle Stan.

Shaun stood still. So did the D'Costas and the neighbourhood.

Sandra flew to Ireland. Months passed by. Shaun still lived in refuge. As if darkness had engulfed his fate, Shaun couldn't find a job either in India or Australia. By this time, all his reserves had drained out, and he was living off the D'Costas.

Joesph D'Costa's son Alfred was planning to migrate to Canada and had found some connections who could help him. So the first step was a passport. Since Shaun was already experienced and had worked in a foreign land, Uncle Joseph requested Shaun to help Alfred with his passport. Those days getting a passport was as tough as getting a housing loan.

Alfred gave Shaun 500 rupees and the passport form with all documents to be deposited at the regional passport office.

It was drizzling. Shaun decided to stand under the shade of an eatery till the rain stopped. The rain graduated to a thunderstorm. Shaun decided to get inside the eatery as he was carrying Alfred's passport application documents.

Since, he couldn't just block a cover, he asked for a cup of tea.

After a long time, Shaun found a moment to spend with himself. He was penniless and was living off charity. All their belongings were sold off, and he was left with just a few clothes and some documents.

The chef inside had just set the tandoor and hung well-marinated mutton *boti kebabs* for *kathi rolls* that the city is known for. The aroma of the burnt edges of the kebabs filled the eatery while the rain got heavier.

Though Shaun lived with the D'Costas, he would spend most of his time outside in search of a job and mostly wouldn't eat over the guilt of being a liability. He would usually pretend that he had had his meals outside. Once in a while Mrs D'Costa would force him to have dinner with them.

Shaun had not eaten well for a long time now. The aroma of the kebabs was too tempting for a hungry Shaun. The desire to have a *kathi roll* tore his mind apart. But the money was not his and was meant to be deposited as Alfred's passport fee.

The chef took out the skewers from the tandoor and hung them inside a glass pane right in front of Shaun. Unable to bear his hunger and the desire to have some good food, Shaun ordered for a mutton kathi roll.

He had one. Then he ordered for another. He had the second and ordered the third. The three kathi rolls and a cup of tea cost him more than half the money that he had with him.

By this time, the rain had stopped, and the road was flooded. His guilt was killing him. Shaun had no clue what to do.

What would he say to the D'Costas? How would be pay Alfred's passport fee?

Shaun walked over to a public park and sat on a bench. He had no clue about what to do and the guilt was tearing him apart.

He was not in a position to share the truth with D'Costas, nor could he live with the truth.

The sun went down. Shaun was still sitting on the bench. Unsure.

He returned to the D'Costas and told them that he had deposited the fees through a friend's father who was a travel agent and would get the receipt in a couple of days. He had hidden the form in a small belt pouch that he had.

Shaun spent the night thinking what to do. Where could he go? Alfred was not sure if Shuan was telling the truth. So when everybody went to sleep, Alfred got hold of Shaun's belt pouch and went to the terrace to find his passport form in it, crumbled to fit in the small space of the pouch.

Next morning was the most embarrassing moment in Shaun's life. Alfred asked him to get out of the house and took back a pair of denims that Uncle Joseph had gifted Shaun.

Alfred pushed the young Gardener out of his house and the building. Shaun didn't know how to react. He hung his head in shame and walked off with tears in his eyes.

All the respect and the warmth for the Gardeners flew out of the window, and for years there was no news of Shaun.

By this time Sandra had married an Irish bookseller and had shifted to Belfast. She had given birth to a baby boy and visited India after her British citizenship was confirmed. She couldn't even trace her brother.

A decade passed by.

The D'Costa family had migrated to Canada. The building was bought over by a Marwari builder called Jai Kishen Murli Lal Murrarka. Most of the old neighbours had left.

When some old-timers met over a drink, the story of the decadence of the Gardeners and Shaun being behind the bars was usually the focal point of gossip.

The jaalfrezi or the beef roast had graduated to *pao bhaji* or *gobi masala,* and the plum cake to *motichur laddos.* Aunty Brown was called *mausiji* and Maureen McMillan was called Mili by the neighbourhood.

Culture had changed with time. Nobody played the guitar any more and sang. One could only hear popular Hindi 'item' songs with some local political goons dancing at the entrance of the building, making it often difficult for the young women to pass by. Nobody shared food, and nobody went for the Sunday Mass. Times had really changed.

Another five years passed by. Still there was no news of Shaun.

The building was demolished. There stood eight sprawling apartments. Seven apartments were occupied while nobody lived in the eighth.

The owner actually lived in London and had bought the apartment through an agent. All paperwork was done, and payments were made in full. Only the court registration of the property was due.

It was monsoons and was raining cats and dogs. The sky was overcast. A black Bentley taxi was struggling to drive through a water-clogged lane. It stopped in front of a modest eatery that had a glass pane with mutton *boti kebabs* hanging on skewers.

The Bentley almost blocked the lane with other cars honking to find a way. A middle-aged gentleman got out and walked through the clogged water, much to the surprise of the people around, and got into the eatery.

It was Shaun after fifteen years.

He had found shelter at the Salvation Army and then had migrated to London, where he first worked as a shopkeeper with a Bangladeshi grocery store in Brick Lane.

Years later and after a series of events, he started a publishing house. His business had flourished, making him one of the richest migrants from India living in West London.

Shaun ordered for three mutton *boti kathi rolls* and a cup of tea. He paid the bill and asked the owner how many support staff he had in the eatery.

Shaun gave each of them 500 rupees as tips and walked through the water-clogged street with his Bentley taxi driver confused over the behaviour of his uber-rich passenger.

The middle-aged Gardener asked the driver to wait in a nearby parking lot while he walked to the public park and sat on the bench that he had sat on helplessly fifteen years back. Memories and thoughts bombarded his matured mind.

The owner of the eatery and his support staff had no clue who the man was and why he had paid each of them 500 rupees.

The next morning, Shaun went to the court to register the eighth apartment in his name. After the court process was over, the Bentley pulled up at the entrance of the new building.

Shaun took the lift and went to the top floor. He turned left and stood still in front of the door of his apartment with tears trickling down his cheeks.

A wooden board at the entrance read 'The Garden of Eden'.

Another year passed.

It was spring in Vancouver. The city looked gorgeous. It looked vibrant with white-and-pink cherry blossoms and celebrations all around: concerts downtown, whale-watching trips departing from Granville Island, kayaking, hiking, and the Cherry Blossom festival itself.

The doorbell rang in a small two-room apartment in Downtown East End, an area with persistent drug, prostitution, and HIV issues in Vancouver with a large number of homeless people.

A delivery boy from a courier service stood with his cap on and an envelope in hand. The door opened, and an elderly man came out.

The sender's name was 'Garden of Eden' and the address was extremely familiar. The elderly man sat on a sofa, turned the television off, put on his reading glasses, and opened the envelope.

It had two Western Union international money transfer receipts and passwords or money transfer control numbers.

The first was in the name of Joseph D'Costa. The amount was 500 Canadian dollars. The second was for Alfred D'Costa, and the amount was for 500,000 Canadian dollars.

The courier had a small note that read 'Five hundred I owe you, Uncle Joseph. Sorry but I was hungry that day, and 500,000 is what your share of profit is, after having invested your 500 in my business . . . Shall ever be grateful for giving me shelter. Best, Shaun Gardener'.

. . . The guilt continues but now in Vancouver!

The Narialpaniwala

Ajay Singh's humble shop selling green coconut water was being flooded with gifts and life-changing promises. People stopped to give a water-cooler and some gave him money too.

Ajay went back home that night richer by a few thousands.

It was not Diwali where he had won some bonanza, nor it was a campaign for any product. So what was happening?

The story goes back a little in time.

Ajay was a blind hard-working young man who would sell coconuts near an expensive set of condominiums in

Gurgaon. Though the apartments ran into crores, cattle once in a while ran into the compound, scared by the speeding cars, and were chased out.

Ajay had lost his vision last year in an accident in the factory where he worked. Doctors had hope that with time and medication he could regain his vision, though partially.

He didn't have anybody to support him at work. His brother would drop him at the shop in the morning and would reluctantly come to pick him up at around midnight. Ajay's mother, who lived in a close-by village would make rotis and some *bhindi sabzi* and pack it in a tiffin box for her son for lunch.

Ajay earned a modest 500 rupees a day till a friend gave him an idea to attract attention.

A life-sized cut-out of a woman in bikini with a green coconut in hand was put up. It was taken from a Jamaican advertisement for rum, enlarged, and pasted on a cardboard.

A skirt was glued around the waist. Moment the wind got stronger or a car passed by at high speed, the skirt would fly up.

It almost gave a Marilyn Monroe effect, which attracted a lot of attention. The innovative idea to sell coconut water caught the attention of local print media, which soon carried small articles on Ajay's otherwise humble shop, which had just four poles and a canvas on top.

Some stories had headlines like 'The Blind man with a Vision' while some sleaze wrote 'The lady with Green Coconuts'. Soon it became a fad to stop by at Ajay's to have coconut water.

Late night, expensive sports cars would pull up while during the day, there were always a couple of expensive sedans that would stop for some green coconut water.

Ajay soon had a fixed clientele. Some would buy coconuts and carry them home while most liked to stop by to drink it there. The best was that Ajay had a big thermocol box filled with ice where he kept the coconuts cool in the scorching heat of North-Indian summers.

He had a box where he requested his customers to drop the money while there was a basket to throw the used coconuts by the side.

Usually, the customers chose the coconut from the thermocol box and gave it to Ajay, who would chop the head part off and make a square hole where he would drop in a paper straw. He charged thirty rupees for each coconut.

This caught the attention of an organisational leadership development consultant, Rajesh Bose, who was running some real-time 'out of the box' experiments to understand human behaviour.

Rajesh stopped by to have coconut water at Ajay's one day. A friend, Feroze Daruwala, who was a short filmmaker, accompanied him.

Rajesh used his neuro-linguistic programming skills and got Ajay to agree to a plan. And what was the plan?

Feroze would set up battery-powered cameras with spy microphones camouflaged in Ajay's shop; the cameras would cover 180 degrees of view facing the road. The idea was to record the behavioural patterns of people who would stop by at the shop. The experiment would run for a couple of months.

Rajesh's idea initially was of no interest to Ajay, but the former promised him a good amount of money. Ajay had to pay for the renovation of his home in his village; besides, he needed money for the treatment for his eyes. So he reluctantly agreed on the basis that somebody from Rajesh's team would always be there in case he ran into trouble.

Salim Shekhar, a liquor baron who lived close by would drive in his expensive red sports car around 11.30 p.m. and stop by for coconut water almost thrice a week. He would mix a good quantity of alcohol in the coconut water and drink it inside the car and would put on some sensuous Latino music; most of the time he would have a new attractive lady with him.

Salim and the ladies always drank out of one coconut, getting them closer to feel the warmth in their breath. It wouldn't be a surprise, if he kissed some of the ladies as Ajay was blind, which was non-intrusive to the flamboyant man's midnight rendezvous.

Ajay was blind but not deaf, and the moans and the groans were enough for him to feel uncomfortable.

The flamboyant liquor baron would chuck the empty coconut right outside the basket and throw a fifty-rupee-note in the box, while after a kiss, some ladies would throw used tissue papers after wiping their smudged lipsticks in the box meant for money.

Salim usually laughed at such pranks of his ladies.

One of Rajesh's support staff had set up a small makeshift cigarette stall and kept an eye from a distance.

Jaggu, a taxi driver would stop by every second day, as his stand was close. He loved the *malai* more than the water, which was so heavy that many a times he skipped lunch.

Jaggu was a sixty-year-old man and was compassionate towards Ajay. He always advised Ajay to get an assistant, something he couldn't afford with his 500 rupees income a day.

Jaggu always gave whatever extra coins he had in his pocket along with thirty rupees for each coconut and never mentioned about the tips to Ajay.

All this was being recorded by the cameras camouflaged in Ajay's shop. Rajesh and Feroze would drop by late at night when Ajay would be wrapping up. They would take the footage and set the camera up for the next day.

Nobody knew what was happening. And this went on for a while.

Gopal Mishra, a fifty-year-old software engineer from IIT with a B school degree often came to Ajay's. Gopal would spend more time talking to Ajay than drinking coconut water. Soon they started talking about their families and personal lives.

'*Sirji*, what do you do? Do you make computers since you are an engineer?' asked Ajay one evening.

'No . . . I always wanted design software but then became a salesman . . . Now I run an American company who sell medical policies with the back-end in many countries,' explained Gopal.

'Are you a manager, *sirji?*' innocently inquired Ajay.

'Yes . . . I am a kind of a manager, Ajay. I am the CEO of the company . . . I mean . . . (pause) . . . I am the boss,' Gopal said reluctantly.

'You must be earning so much of money . . . I wish I could learn how to make computers,' sighed Ajay.

It's a known fact that people who are otherwise physically challenged have highly developed senses. Ajay's hearing and olfactory sensibilities were extremely strong. By the sound of the car, he would know if it was Salim or Gopal or Jaggu. And by the smell, he could tell that a new woman was in Salim's car!

A senior professional from Gopal's company, Mehul, too would come to have coconut water. He would come with his young son and wife, usually after dinner.

They would park their expensive SUV and walk around for a little while and then have coconut water and head back home. This was almost a daily routine when Mehul was not travelling.

Mehul was extremely aggressive and rude. His temperament hung on a thin string, and he would not stop to misbehave in front of his seven-year-old son.

'Don't you think you are taking advantage of your disability? You are selling each coconut for thirty rupees whereas it should be twenty. You think I am a fool like the other customers of yours?' shouted Mehul aggressively at Ajay one night.

'I buy it for twenty each, *sirji* . . . since I am blind, I cant go to the *mandi* to buy . . . Instead, they deliver here at an additional cost . . . Don't you think I should make Rs. 10 out of each sale . . . or else, how do I eat my meals, *sirji*?' politely replied Ajay.

'So you are putting your meals on my bloody head . . . This is the problem with you poor people. Moment you see a rich man, you want to eat out of his plate . . . I know people in the police. I can have you evicted from here . . . Never mind, here is the money,' Mehul grumbled and drove off with his family after having three coconuts.

Before getting into the car, Mehul dropped a fifty-rupee-note and took a twenty out when he had to pay ninety.

Rajesh and Firoze would come very night and take the footage back and set the cameras for the next day.

After a week, a familiar sound of a car approached Ajay's shop. He knew it was Gopal.

'How are you, *sirji*?' asked a happy Ajay.

'I am good, Ajay. How has been business?' inquired Gopal.

'Better than before though I find it difficult to handle rude customers,' said a thoughtful Ajay.

'*Sirji* . . . can I ask you something please?' requested the young coconut water vendor.

'You must be getting so much of money. I hear big managers in big companies get lakhs of rupees as salary . . . but why do you drive a small car which is mostly used as a taxi? I mean, you can buy the best of cars!' hesitantly asked Ajay.

Gopal smiled and said, 'True, my friend. My hatchback is the most popular taxi in India. I can actually buy the best car. If I ask my company, there will be a new car at my doorstep in no time . . . (pause) . . . but, Ajay, tell me something, isn't it a crime to drive an expensive car when right outside your window, more than 90 per cent of the people don't get a proper meal . . . I cant sit in the lap of luxury of top-end cars when little children right outside are begging for food . . . Ajay, the development of Gurgaon is not the face of true India. It pains me to see so much of inequality.'

Mahinder ran a property company where he dealt with high-end corporate rentals. His office was almost right next to the condominiums, and many a times, he walked to Ajay's for coconut water. He would always wear a white shirt, a pair of white trousers, and white sandals.

Mahinder never paid a single penny ever. He would throw the coconut right in front of the shop and walk back. Many a times, he would pull out a tenner from Ajay's box of money to buy a cigarette from the stall next and blew nicotine while walking back with the feeling that Ajay owed him the coconut and the cigarette since he was the local politician's nephew and carried a licensed gun.

Once at midnight, Mahinder came terribly drunk. He put five coconuts in a row right in the middle of the road on the divider. He pulled out his gun and shot each one of them.

'Your coconuts are good to practise my aim once in a while,' shouted the drunk man while walking back.

A shocked Ajay stood still. He knew it was pointless to have a conversation.

Mahesh Bhalla was a sales manager for an upcoming cell phone company. He had to visit some markets in the area for work, and while going back, he would stop for some coconut water at Ajay's.

'I get a lot of free phones for promotion . . . I will give you one . . . besides, my friend is the head of Ophthalmology at the new hospital that has opened here . . . I will recommend you so that you can go and consult him for your eyes free of cost . . . and I will also speak to our canteen manager. I will help you to supply coconut water in my company this summer . . . Your life will change, Ajay . . . I generally don't help people. But I will for you.' Bhalla never failed to tell Ajay how well connected he was and how with his connections, he could change Ajay's life.

'*Arrre yaar*, if I can help you so much without any interest . . . I am sure you can give me some discount.' Mahesh would manipulate.

Ajay would politely smile.

The process went on. And every day Rajesh and Feroze would come at night and collect the footage. They soon started editing them and made a short film called *Narialpaniwala*. They collated the guerilla shooting of real-life human behavioural patterns caught off guard.

This was when Feroze came up with a brilliant idea. He suggested that Ajay should share the raw footage with some of the regular customers and have the cameras study their individual reaction. Rajesh immediately approved.

Both went and told Ajay about the plan and promised to pay a total of Rs. 10,000.

The blind coconut water vendor shared the short film with Salim, Mehul, Gopal, Mahinder, Jaggu, Mahesh, and some other regular customers of his.

The cameras and the microphones were still in position.

Ajay would say, '*Sirji,* one director from Mumbai has made a movie on me. I am the hero . . . It has your photos too . . . please watch it.' And he handed a CD to each of them.

Most would be taken aback knowing their 'photos' were in the film and all would ask, 'How come my photo? Where did you get it from?'

'I am a blind man. The cinema people know. But please do see, *sirji*' would be Ajay's standard reply.

Everybody went back and watched *Narialpaniwala* and was in utter shock. They all failed to contemplate how they were captured in the frames.

Now the reaction of each was different.

Salim went to Ajay's in a black sedan instead of his flamboyant red sports car and got down with someone who apparently looked like his wife. His driver carried a box just behind them. Salim was wearing a pair of denims and a white kurta on top with a pair of slippers.

He and his wife had coconut water. Salim asked his driver to give the box to Ajay.

'Your coconuts are so good. You must make a permanent structure here. I have a gift for you.' Salim gave a packet containing 10,000 rupees to Ajay and told him that in the box was a water cooler.

'You have treated me to such refreshing coconut water so many times in the terrible summer of North India . . . while you drank water that was as good as hot in the scorching sun. From now, you will drink cold water.' Salim got into the car and drove off even before Ajay could react.

'Son, you must have an assistant. How will you manage? Your business seems to be growing. . . . You need help,' advised Jaggu while sharing lunch with him followed by coconut water.

Jaggu didn't forget to drop all the coins he had in his pockets in the box for money after having paid thirty rupees.

Mahinder walked in one night completely drunk.

'You have made me a hero, lad . . . I look good firing coconuts in the middle of the road . . . I look like a glorious man.' Mahinder took out his gun and threw a coconut in air and fired.

He then took out a tenner from Ajay's box of money and walked back after buying a cigarette. He sang an old song from the 1960s and blew rings in the air.

Mehul never returned, ashamed of himself, while Mahesh came back the next week again asking for discounts after promising the sky for Ajay.

Gopal came one night and thanked Ajay for showing the actual face of Mehul. But he shared that he was disappointed with the footage being shot without consent.

'Whenever you take somebody's photograph, you must ask for consent, Ajay . . . I understand you need money. Would you mind if I give you some for your eye treatment?' asked Gopal.

Now Rajesh and Feroze had more footage to assess how people react when exposed to their natural characteristics.

But their project was not complete without some footage of Ajay sharing his experiences. So Feroze went back. Ajay was not in the shop and his brother was selling coconut water in his place.

'Where is Ajay?' asked Feroze.

'He is unwell and will take more than a month to recover,' informed Ajay's brother.

Both Rajesh and Feroze would drive past Ajay's shop expecting him to return for the final footage.

After over a month's waiting, they found Ajay at the shop.

'What happened to you? Your brother wouldn't disclose anything. Hope you are well,' inquired Rajesh.

'Never mind that . . . where is the money that you promised to give me?' demanded Ajay.

Feroze told him that they would shoot some footage with Ajay's point of view, and then they would give the money.

'I need money. So you first pay, and then I will talk.' Ajay sounded determined.

Rajesh and Feroze had no choice.

'Here . . . take this packet. This has 10,000. Hope you are happy . . . Can we talk now?' asked Rajesh.

They shot a footage about how Ajay felt and reacted to different situations with different people behaving differently.

'Thank you, Ajay. It's been a good journey. Hope the money comes handy in life,' smiled Rajesh while he and Feroze walked towards their car.

'Sirji, how can you leave not having some coconut water? I am a poor man, but let me too give you a gift. Please have some coconut water and take a few for home,' invited Ajay.

Rajesh and Feroze turned back and drank a coconut each.

While they walked back, Ajay called them out again.

'*Sirji*, for the past one month I was in Vellore. I have been under medication for a while now. My eyes are getting better, and I can partially see. . . . (pause) . . . good enough to check that you gave me 1,000 in the packet and lied saying that it had 10,000 . . .'

Rajesh and Feroze stood still in shame. Shocked.

Rajesh quickly reached in his pockets and took out 9,000 and went closer to Ajay.

'I think it was a mistake in counting. Please take this money. And we are so happy that you can see now,' Rajesh said, his voice trembling.

'I may be poor but am not a fool. You can keep the money. And the 1,000 that you gave too . . . Also I have camouflaged my friend's video camera, which has shot this entire conversation . . . Please come tomorrow for the footage . . . Gopal *sirji* will help me to do that . . . It will help you to sum up your study on human behaviour,' smiled Ajay while both men hung their heads in shame and walked towards their car, never to return again.